Clint reached  rew
his hand back   the
man's right ha   around behind his
back at an unnatural angle.

Bell looked at Clint and said, "Butting your nose
in where it don't belong, ain't ya, mister?"

"I don't know," Clint said. He was holding Lukas
with his left hand so that his gun hand was still free.

"You against the four of us?" Bell asked,
laughing.

Clint looked down at Lukas then pulled up on his
arm until they all heard something pop. He released
the arm which fell uselessly to the man's side. Lukas
cradled it and cursed.

"One against three," Clint said.

Bell turned and squinted at Clint, studying him for
a few moments, then he looked at Starr. "Help Lukas
up. We're leavin'. We got to get him to a doctor."

Bell looked at Clint and pointed a finger. "I'm
Bell. You and me will meet again . . ."

DON'T MISS THESE
ALL-ACTION WESTERN SERIES
FROM THE BERKLEY PUBLISHING GROUP

THE GUNSMITH by J. R. Roberts
Clint Adams was a legend among lawmen, outlaws, and ladies. They called him . . . the Gunsmith.

LONGARM by Tabor Evans
The popular long-running series about U.S. Deputy Marshal Long—his life, his loves, his fight for justice.

SLOCUM by Jake Logan
Today's longest-running action Western. John Slocum rides a deadly trail of hot blood and cold steel.

McMASTERS by Lee Morgan
The blazing new series from the creators of *Longarm*. When McMasters shoots, he shoots to kill. To his enemies, he is the most dangerous man they have ever known.

THE GUNSMITH

168

THE FRENCH MODELS

J. R. ROBERTS

J

JOVE BOOKS, NEW YORK

THE FRENCH MODELS

A Jove Book / published by arrangement with
the author

PRINTING HISTORY
Jove edition / December 1995

ISBN: 0-515-11767-6

A JOVE BOOK®
Jove Books are published by The Berkley Publishing Group,
200 Madison Avenue, New York, New York 10016.
JOVE and the "J" design are trademarks
belonging to Jove Publications, Inc.

PRINTED IN THE UNITED STATES OF AMERICA

10 9 8 7 6 5 4 3 2 1

ONE

Clint noticed the three women right away.

He was on San Francisco's Barbary Coast doing a favor for a friend. When he told Rick Hartman in Labyrinth, Texas, that he was heading for San Francisco, Rick asked if he'd deliver something. . . .

"Sure. What is it?"

"A package."

"What kind of package?"

"A small one. You'll be able to carry it easy. Are you taking your rig?"

"No," Clint said, "just Duke." He'd been traveling less and less those days with his rig, which contained his gunsmithing tools, and team. He wondered if the time would come when he would give up gunsmithing for good. It just seemed that lately when he traveled it was with a certain destination in mind, and he needed to get there faster than his wagon would allow him.

"Why are you going to San Francisco?" Rick asked.

"No particular reason," Clint said. "I just feel like going."

Clint had been to San Francisco many times in the past. He had friends there, and places where he was known— hotels, saloons, gambling establishments—and it was a place where men attempted to shoot him from ambush only on occasion. That happened more on the trail than in a city the size of San Francisco.

Clint had often thought that if he ever truly settled down to live in one place it would be a city like San Francisco, or Denver, or New York. Maybe even Chicago. He wasn't quite ready to settle down, though.

"What's in the package?" Clint asked.

"Is that important?" Rick asked.

Clint frowned.

"No, it's not important. I'm just curious."

"Well . . ."

"Is there a problem with telling me what's in the package?" Clint asked, a bit testily. "I mean, if there is, just say so and I won't ask again."

"Well . . . there's not a problem with me, really, but there might be with the fella at the other end."

"And who is the fellow at the other end?" Clint asked. "Can you tell me that?"

"Of course I can tell you that," Rick said. "How else would you know who to give it to?"

"Hey, I'm just asking," Clint said. "Apparently there are some questions I just can't ask. . . . "

"Look, don't get testy. The man at the other end is Eddie Garland. Do you know him?"

"Garland?" Clint thought a moment. "I don't think so. Should I?"

Rick shrugged.

"Just thought you might have run across him a time or two. Used to do his business in Texas before he picked up stakes and moved to San Francisco."

"His name doesn't sound familiar."

"Well, he's got a place on the Barbary Coast. It's called the Red Wave or something nautical like that. You'll find it."

"And all you want me to do is give him this package?"

"Right."

"A small package."

"Right."

"And you won't tell me what's in it?"

"I think I'll leave that up to him, if that's okay with you."

Clint had the package, which was wrapped in plain brown paper, in his left hand as he walked along the Coast. He'd shaken it a few times along the way between Texas and San Francisco, but shaking it had offered him no clue to its contents. Truth be told, by this time he didn't really care what was in it.

He saw the women first. He noticed them because they were not exactly dressed for being outside. There were three of them, one with blond hair, one with brown hair, and one with black skin. They were across the way, their backs to the water, and seemed to be posing. He squinted and moved closer, saw that they were all very beautiful in their own way. They were wearing filmy, gauzy clothing that seemed to be more suited to the inside of a bordello than a Barbary Coast dock.

He didn't see the man for a few moments, but when he did he understood. He was a tall, gaunt man standing in front of an easel, working with a brush and paints. It didn't take a genius to figure out that he was a painter and the women were his models. It also didn't take a big brain to figure out that setting up here on the dock with those three women was asking for trouble, and while he watched, trouble approached. Four men had crossed the street and were nudging each other as they headed over.

Clint decided not to butt in if he didn't have to, and leaned against a pole to watch. Maybe they were just curious about what the man was doing. Or maybe they wanted their portraits painted and were going to make the artist an offer.

And maybe they were just what they looked like . . . trouble.

TWO

The painter's name was Henri LeConte. He and his three models had just gotten off a boat the day before, from France. He had persuaded the three women to come to America with him so that he could paint them against the backdrop of the American West.

The brown-haired girl was Gabrielle. She answered to Gaby. She was twenty-nine and had a wonderful wide mouth that smiled a lot. She was the larger, more full-bodied of the three models. In fact, she was just a tad over five foot eight while neither of the other women were taller than five four. LeConte liked the difference in height.

The blonde was Marie. She had a luscious full-lipped mouth and red lipstick that often looked smudged. She was twenty-two, five four, and slender. Gaby teased her about how thin she was, and how her own waist measurement was larger than the blonde's bust measurement.

The black girl was Jolie. She was twenty-four with long, jet black hair and full lips. She was not as full-bodied as Gaby but certainly carried more curves than Marie did.

LeConte did not see the four men crossing the street, but the three women did.

"Henri—" Gaby said, but he interrupted her.

"Not now."

"Henri—" Marie tried, but was given the same treatment.

"Not now, Marie."

The four men heard the exchange and realized that the women and man were speaking with foreign accents.

"Ain't no more slaves in this country, Frenchy," Harvey Bell called out. He recognized the accent because he had once known a trapper who talked funny like that.

Harvey Bell stopped just behind LeConte, and the other three men also stopped. They were called Starr, Lukas, and John—his last name. All four men were clad in trail-worn clothes and had ridden into San Francisco several days ago together. Since then they had been looking for women and/or trouble. In this situation they seemed to have found both.

Starr, Lukas, and John stood with their arms folded across their chests. They were content to let Bell do the talking, while they ogled the women.

The three women pulled their gauzy garments around their bodies, covering themselves as well as they could from the prying eyes of the men. They were women, they didn't mind being admired by men, but *these* men were devouring them with their eyes, not just looking.

LeConte said, without turning, "Not now."

Bell looked over LeConte's shoulder at the canvas,

which at the moment was a mass of colors with indistinguishable shapes.

"That don't look like nothin'," Bell said.

LeConte stopped now and looked over his shoulder in annoyance. He had very pale skin, a small, well-cared-for goatee, and eyes that would have been beautiful on any woman. Those eyes were now, however, narrowed and accusatory.

"Monsieur," he said, "I would appreciate you not looking over my shoulder, please."

"What the hell did he call you?" Starr asked.

"He called him 'Monsoor,' " Lukas said. "That's French talk."

"How do you know?" Starr demanded.

"I heard it before on a French whore," Lukas said.

"Shut up," Bell said to them.

LeConte had turned his attention back to his canvas, ignoring the men.

"This pretty Frenchman is ignoring us, boys," Bell said. "Whataya think of that?"

"Pretty dang rude," John said.

Starr and Lukas were in their twenties, while John was in his mid-forties. They all followed Bell, though, who had just turned thirty several days earlier.

"That's what I say," Bell said. He tapped LeConte on the shoulder. "Hey, Frenchy. Me and my friends think you're bein' real rude."

Starr nudged Lukas and said, "Let's get a closer look at them women."

Lukas said, "That French whore I was with like to turned me inside out. Maybe these gals will oblige, huh?"

"We might as well ask 'em," Starr said.

They walked away while John remained standing behind Bell, arms still folded across his chest.

"Please," LeConte said, "I beg you, I must not lose the light."

Bell reached over LeConte's shoulder as if to touch the paint on the canvas. Faster than he could follow, the artist caught him around the wrist in a tight grip. The first time Bell tried to pull away he couldn't. He yanked harder and LeConte let him go, causing him to stagger back into John.

"Son of a—"

"Do not touch the canvas," LeConte said. This time he turned around fully to face Bell and the other man. It was then he noticed that the other two had moved. He turned and saw Starr and Lukas over by the women, talking to them, poking and prodding at them.

"This one's a big one," Starr said, poking Gaby on the arm. "I like big girls. Whataya say, señorita?"

"Señorita is Spanish, you idiot, not French."

"Whatever. It's foreign, ain't it? Whataya say?"

"Please," Gaby said, her English not as accented as LeConte's, "leave us alone."

"You ladies must be cold," Lukas said, eyeing Marie appreciatively. He liked small women, himself. "We could warm you up some, if you like."

"We do not like," Jolie said. She was less fearful of the men than Gaby and Marie. She pushed Lukas away forcefully.

Laughing, Lukas looked at Starr and said, "Feisty, ain't she?"

"Yeah, but she can't be French."

"Why not?"

"Because she's black."

"So?"

"So, you ever seen a black French gal?"

"Hey," Lukas said, "she talks Frenchy-like, so she probably is."

LeConte looked over to where Starr and Lukas were pawing and prodding the girls and said to Bell, "Tell your friends not to bother the girls."

"Oh, I can't tell my friends anything," Bell said, "especially when it comes to women."

"Then I will tell them myself."

Bell smiled and said, "Go ahead."

LeConte walked away from Bell, who looked over at John and smiled. The older man did not smile back.

THREE

"I still say she can't be no French whore," Starr said.

"Why not? Look at the way she's dressed."

Marie took offense.

"These are not whore's clothes."

"Hey, I been in a lot of whorehouses, lady," Lukas said, "and them's whore's clothes."

"Why don't you leave us alone?" Jolie demanded.

"You know," Starr said, "if you girls come with us we could make you nice and warm. You must be cold in them clothes."

"Whore's clothes," Lukas said.

"They are not!" Marie shouted.

Lukas laughed, taking great pleasure in upsetting the little blonde. It made her face red and she looked real pretty that way.

"I think you and me are gonna get along swell," he said to her, grabbing her by the wrist.

"Let her go!" Jolie shouted.

"You heard the lady," Henri LeConte said.

Lukas turned his head just in time to see LeConte reach

out for him. The artist closed his hand around the man's wrist and exerted pressure.

"Ow, what the—" Lukas said, releasing his hold on Marie because the pain was so intense.

"Now you must go awa—" LeConte started, but he never finished.

"Look out!" the three women shouted in unison, but it was too late. Something crashed into LeConte from behind and he felt himself flying through the air. When he hit the water he disappeared from view.

"I hope he can swim," Bell said.

Marie swore at him in French, and then looked shocked at herself.

"I don't know what she said, Bell," Lukas said, "but it sounded bad."

"It might have been bad," Bell said, "but it sounded pretty." He reached out and grabbed Marie's arm. "You gals can come with us now."

"Yeah," Starr said, grabbing Gaby's arm. She was not only a big girl, but she was strong, too, and she resisted.

Lukas had wanted the blonde, but now that Bell had taken hold of her he grabbed the black girl's arm. She reached out with her other hand and scratched his face.

"You bitch!" he shouted and drew back his right hand to strike her.

It never landed.

Clint didn't start across the street until he saw the two men approach the women and begin to paw them. He still moved slowly, though, watching the action. It wasn't until the artist was knocked into the water that he started to run. He reached the group just as one of them drew his hand back to strike the black girl.

He grabbed the man's right hand and twisted it around behind his back at an unnatural angle, creating tremendous pressure at the shoulder.

"Hey, ow, Jesus—" Lukas said, staggering back and then going to one knee.

Bell looked at Clint and said, "Butting your nose in where it don't belong, ain't ya, mister?"

"I don't know," Clint said. He was holding Lukas with his left hand so that his gun hand was still free. It never occurred to him that to do this he must have dropped Rick Hartman's package along the way.

"You against the four of us?" Bell asked, laughing.

Clint looked down at Lukas then pulled up on his arm until they all heard something pop. He released the arm, which fell uselessly to the man's side. Lukas cradled it and cursed.

"One against three," Clint said.

"Three's plenty," Bell said, releasing Marie's arm. Starr was still holding Gaby's, but his eyes were on Bell, waiting for a signal.

"Bell."

The man turned and looked at John.

"Let it go."

"Why?"

"I'll tell you later."

Bell turned and squinted at Clint, studying him for a few moments, then he looked at Starr.

"Help Lukas up. We're leavin'. We got to get him to a doctor."

"What? But, Bell—"

"Just do it."

Starr reluctantly released Gaby and helped Lukas to his feet. He staggered past Bell, trying to support his friend's weight.

"You could help—" Starr said to John, but the man ignored him.

Bell looked at Clint and pointed a finger.

"I'm Bell. You and me will meet again."

"I'm at your service, anytime," Clint said.

Bell said, "Yeah, yeah," then turned and followed Lukas and Starr.

Clint looked at the older man and saw that he was still watching him. He seemed familiar, but Clint couldn't place him. He fixed the man's description in his mind so that he might ask someone later.

They stared at each other for a few moments, and then the man turned and followed the other three.

It was then that Clint remembered the man in the water.

FOUR

"I hope your friend can swim," he said to the women.

"Henri!" they shouted, as if they all had just remembered him, too.

The four of them looked into the water but did not see anyone.

"Can he swim?" Clint asked.

"Yes, he can," Jolie said.

"H-help," they heard a voice call.

Clint leaned over so that he could take a steeper look down, and there was the artist, clinging to the dock pilings.

"Grab my legs," Clint said to the women as he laid down.

"What?" Marie asked.

"Grab his legs," Jolie said, as she and Gaby proceeded to do the same.

Supported by the weight of the women, Clint leaned over further and further until he could reach the artist. The man closed his hand over Clint's wrist in a surprisingly firm grip, and Clint followed suit. Holding each other that way he pulled the man up to the dock, where he flopped onto his back with the girls gathered around him.

Clint stood up and dried his hand on his pants. Gaby looked up at him, then stood up while the other two continued to check the artist to see if he was all right.

"We are very grateful to you." He found himself liking her accent, the way she spoke.

"That's all right." Suddenly he looked down at his hands.

"What is it?" she asked.

"I had a small package in my hand," he said, looking around on the ground. "I must have dropped it."

"We will help you find it."

"That's okay—"

"Please," he heard the artist say, "I am all right. Let me up."

Clint stepped over and extended his hand down to the man. They grabbed each other's wrists as they had before and he helped the man to his feet.

"*Merci*. Thank you," the man said.

"Our rescuer has lost a package," Gaby said to the others. "We must help him find it."

"What does it look like?" Marie asked. Now that the trouble was over she was batting her eyes at Clint. They were very pretty eyes, clear and blue.

"It's about this big, wrapped in plain brown paper."

"We will find it," she said, and the three women fanned out.

"I am Henri LeConte," the artist said, and they shook hands.

"My name is Clint Adams."

"We are grateful that you came to help when you did. Had I not been knocked into the water . . ."

"I know," Clint said, "you could have handled it yourself."

"I do not think so," the man said honestly, "not all four, anyway." Suddenly, he looked stricken. "My canvas."

He hurried over to where his paints and easel were. Apparently as they left Bell had stomped it all into the ground.

"I'm sorry that happened," Clint said.

"Ah, it is not a tragedy," the artist admitted. "I was simply finding the right colors to go with the light."

"Here it is." Clint heard Marie behind him. She was brandishing his package like a small child with a toy. "Is this it?"

"That's it, thank you," he said, taking it from her.

The other girls came over and Clint was suddenly the object of everyone's attention.

"We must go back to the hotel, girls," LeConte said.

"Oh, Henri, we want to talk to . . ."

"Clint," Clint said.

"We want to talk to Clint some more," Gaby said.

"You may talk to him at dinner."

"Dinner?" Clint asked.

"But of course. You must allow us to buy you dinner to show our gratitude," LeConte said.

"That's very nice but—"

"Oh, please," Gaby said, taking his arm.

"Yes, please," Marie said, taking his other arm.

"Well . . . all right, then."

"Good. You will meet us at our hotel?" LeConte asked.

"I will."

"At . . . say, seven?"

"Yes."

"*Bon*," LeConte said, which Clint knew meant "good." "We are staying at the . . . oh, what is it?"

"Mystic Palace," Jolie said.

"On the Barbary Coast," Clint said. "I know it."

"Good, then we shall see you there, eh?" LeConte said.

"You will."

"Good, *mon ami*, good."

LeConte started away, with Jolie trailing. Marie squeezed Clint's arm, batted her eyes at him, and followed.

"What is *mon ami*?" he asked Gaby.

"It means 'my friend.' "

"Oh . . . well, good."

"We are very grateful," she said to him again. She kissed his cheek impulsively, then hurried to catch up to the rest.

He liked that accent.

FIVE

Clint examined the package in his hands. He hoped that he had not damaged what was inside when he dropped it.

He found Garland's place a couple of blocks further on the Coast. It was not called the Red Wave but the Red Haven. He thought he would have liked "Wave" better.

He entered and found himself in a bar, much like any other bar on the Barbary Coast. The floor was peppered with tables, and on the left wall was a pitted bar. Behind the bar was a man who, for want of a better word, looked pitted to match the bar.

It was early evening so Clint was surprised that the place was less then full—much less than full. There was a man sitting at a table, and one at the bar, and that was it for the clientele.

He approached the bar, and the bartender came over.

"Is Garland around?"

"Who's asking?" Up close Clint saw that the man did indeed have a pitted, pockmarked face that made him a perfect match for the bar. He had salt-and-pepper hair and seemed to be in his forties.

"Clint Adams."

"So?"

"Rick Hartman sent me."

Clint couldn't tell from the look on the man's face if either name meant anything to him. He stared at Clint for a few moments more, then looked at the other man at the bar.

"Sammy, go tell the boss."

"Right."

Sammy left a half full beer on the bar and went through a door in the back of the room.

"Want a drink?" the man asked.

"Sure." Clint put the package on the bar.

"What'll you have?"

"Beer."

"Comin' up."

He drew a cold beer and put it in front of Clint, who drank half of it down gratefully.

"You been in the water?" the man asked.

"What?" Clint asked, then looked down at himself. His shirtfront was wet, from lying down on the dock. "Oh, no, I just . . . fell."

"Gotta be careful around here," the bartender said. "Man falls down, might find a lot of men on top of him before he knows it."

"I'll keep that in mind."

The man nodded and started cleaning the bar with a dirty rag.

Clint had a second beer in front of him by the time Sammy came out.

"Boss says to bring him back."

"Go on back, then," the bartender said.

"Thanks." He took a hurried sip of the second beer.

"Take it with you," the bartender said.

"Yeah? Thanks."

Clint picked up the beer and turned to Sammy.

"Lead the way."

Sammy nodded. He was a young man, probably in his early twenties, tall and slender. His age was hidden by the fact that he was filthy, but Clint had a feeling that was by design. In fact, he had the feeling that this whole saloon was a front—and for what, he was about to find out.

SIX

Clint followed the man through the door and down a hallway to another door. Along the way they passed two empty rooms that looked like no one had been in them for a while, cobwebs and all.

When Sammy opened another door all Clint saw was darkness.

"Whoa," he said. "Where are we going?"

Sammy stepped away from the doorway so Clint could see the stairs.

"We're goin' down," he said. "Everythin' is happenin' downstairs."

"Okay," Clint said, satisfied that he wasn't being led into a dark room. At the bottom of the stairs he could see some light.

Sammy took a lamp from a nail on the wall, lit it, and started down with Clint behind him.

When they reached the bottom Clint saw another door. Sammy knocked on it. A man opened it, nodded, and stepped aside to allow them to enter.

In this underground room was all the activity Clint

might have expected to see upstairs, and more. There were all forms of gambling going on, and a full bar in operation with two bartenders who looked like they had their hands full.

"Why underground?" Clint asked Sammy.

The younger man looked at him and said, "It's cooler."

"Where's Garland?"

"In the back," Sammy said. "I'll take you."

Sammy led the way again, this time through the crowd until they reached a door in the back. Along the way Clint noticed that the floor was hard-packed dirt and the ceiling hardwood. The walls were also wood.

"Go ahead in," Sammy said.

"Thanks for the tour."

Sammy shrugged, turned, and walked away. Clint knocked on the door and entered. There was a man standing behind a desk, wearing a suit and tie. When he saw Clint he came from behind the desk, hand extended.

"Clint."

"That's right," Clint said, although it hadn't sounded like a question.

"Ed Garland." They shook hands. "I don't know if you remember but we met once."

"We did?" Clint was embarrassed.

"Ah, I didn't think you'd remember. It was many years ago. Come on in, have a seat. Drink?"

Clint showed Garland the mug in his hand, wondering how the man could have missed it.

"No, I mean a real drink. I've got some good whiskey, and some great brandy—"

"This'll do fine," Clint said.

"Okay, then, have a seat."

"Here's your package." Clint handed it over.

"Thanks a lot," Garland said. He went around his desk, put the package down, and seemed to forget about it. He sat down and smiled at Clint.

He was a tall, slender man, probably in his late thirties, with a close-cropped beard and mustache. Although his hair was dark, his beard seemed more auburn. It was an odd mixture.

"So tell me, how is Rick?"

"He's fine," Clint said. "Aren't you going to open that?"

"There's no need. I know what's in it. Say, your shirt's wet. Did you have some trouble?"

"I had some, yeah, although it wasn't really mine."

"Anything I could help with?" Garland asked.

"No, there's no help needed," Clint said, and then he went ahead and explained what the trouble had been.

"French, huh? He was kind of foolish exposing his models to the element down here."

"I'll tell him that tonight," Clint said. "I'm having dinner with them."

"All of them?"

"Yes."

"Sounds interesting."

Clint sipped his beer.

"This is an interesting setup you have here, Mr. Garland."

"Oh, no," Garland said, "call me Ed, Clint . . . or Eddie, if you prefer."

"Thanks . . . Eddie."

"Is it all right if I call you Clint?"

"Sure."

"Great, great. Say, if you want to do some gambling while you're here . . . where are you staying?"

"That new hotel in Portsmouth Square, the Maxwell."

"Great place. Have you been there before?"

"No."

"But you've been to San Francisco before."

"Many times."

"Then you know your way around."

"Yes," Clint said. "I picked the Maxwell because I've never stayed there before."

"Good choice, good choice. They have excellent gambling there as well, but if you ever feel like coming down here some night you'll be my guest. Food and drink on the house."

"And money to gamble with?"

Garland laughed.

"I'm not that friendly to anyone."

"Can you tell me why your operation is down here rather than upstairs?"

"Simple," Garland said. "I outgrew the upstairs. I didn't know about down here when I bought the place, only discovered it after. Once I got too big for the upstairs this seemed like a natural—and people love coming underground to gamble."

And, Clint had to admit, it was cool.

He stayed long enough to finish his beer, hoping that Garland would open the package, but he never did. When the beer was gone the man told him to leave the mug on his desk and walked him to the door and out where the action was.

Clint saw poker, faro, roulette, dice, red dog, some Chinese games, and a wheel of fortune. That was actually the simplest game of all. Put your money on a number and watch the big wheel go around. There weren't nearly as many numbers as on a roulette wheel, and the odds weren't as high.

Garland walked him to the doorway that led upstairs.

"You're not hiding down here from anyone, are you?" Clint asked.

"Like who? The law? I've got no reason to hide from the law, Clint. No, as I said, the people love it, it's roomy, and you got to admit, it's cooler down here."

"Yeah," Clint said, opening the door, "it sure is."

As Clint left the Red Haven Ed Garland called Sammy to his office. While he waited for him, he sat at his desk and stared at the package Clint Adams had delivered from Rick Hartman. He was still sitting there, staring, when Sammy entered.

"You wanted me, boss?"

"Yes," Garland said. "The man who just left is Clint Adams."

Sammy looked surprised.

"That was the Gunsmith?"

"That's right."

"Whew," Sammy said, "if I'd known that I woulda been nervous."

"I want you to keep an eye on him."

"What for?"

"Because I say so."

Sammy shrugged.

"Well, okay, boss, but I don't think I can catch up to him to follow him now—"

"He's staying at the Maxwell," Garland said.

"If you know where he is, why do I have to find him?" Sammy asked.

"I didn't say I wanted you to find him, Sammy," Garland said patiently. "I said I want you to keep an eye on him. I don't want anything to happen to him. Okay?"

"Okay, boss," Sammy said, "whatever you say."

"Thank you."

SEVEN

Clint went back to his hotel to take a bath before having dinner with Henri LeConte and his three models. Clint had heard stories about French women, and although he could recall having been with some, he thought they had been more Cajun than actual French ladies from France.

Clint had been impressed by the Maxwell as soon as he entered. Every so often he liked to treat himself to a hotel that featured crystal and mahogany, and the Maxwell had plenty of both in evidence right in the lobby. He had taken one of the best rooms, because Rick Hartman had agreed to split the cost with him if he delivered the package to Garland.

Soaking in a hot tub right in his room, Clint thought again about the package. He still wished that Garland had opened it immediately. His curiosity about the package was starting to annoy him, so he decided to think about other things.

That is, three other things.

Gaby . . .

Jolie . . .

Marie . . .

Actually, the model who interested him the least was the slender blonde, Marie. He enjoyed more meat on his women when he had the choice. Gaby interested him because she was a big woman, but he found himself very curious about Jolie, who was both black and French, a combination he had never encountered before.

He wondered about the artist, Henri LeConte. Was he sleeping with one of the models? Or all three? Which woman was his?

He got out of the tub, dried himself off, and started to dress in his best clothes when he remembered that their hotel was on the Barbary Coast. Going there well dressed was an invitation to robbers and thieves to try to take your money and anything else they could get. He put his suit away and dressed instead in clean clothes.

He went downstairs, and in the lobby he could hear the sounds of gambling coming from the casino portion of the hotel: the loud murmur of voices, the sound of the roulette ball bouncing around on the wheel, the click of chips falling on chips. Clint loved gambling but had done none since his arrival in San Francisco last night. After he had checked into the hotel and seen that Duke was taken care of by the hotel livery, he'd had something to eat and then succumbed to exhaustion. Maybe it was a concession to age, but instead of going into the saloon, or going gambling, or looking for a woman, he had gone to bed. The result was that he was well rested today. He could have started gambling now and gone on most of the night, but he'd accepted the French artist's invitation for dinner and intended to keep the date—with the artist and his three beautiful models.

When he reached the hotel where the artist and models were staying, they were in the lobby, attracting a lot of attention. Men and women were standing around them, watching them, studying them. The women were dressed more conventionally now, but that did not make them any less noticeable. Even clothed from head to toe, and even if they were somewhere other than the Barbary Coast, they'd attract attention. LeConte was dressed much as he had been earlier in the day, plain clothes, worse for wear, only now he had added a black cape with a bright red lining.

"Ah, my friend," LeConte said, smiling and spreading his arms, "you have come."

"Yes," Clint said, "I have."

"Clint," Gaby said, "how nice to see you."

Marie came and took his left arm. Jolie stood back, eyeing him suspiciously. Clint wondered if she was suspicious of all men, and if so, why?

Clint looked around at the small crowd that was gathered around them.

"Friends of yours?" he asked.

"We have no friends in this country," LeConte said, "except for you, of course."

"Perhaps we had better leave," Gaby said, "before they decide to do more than watch."

"Good point," Clint said. "Where did you want to eat?"

LeConte shrugged and said, "We have been eating

here, and the food is terrible.''

"Then you should eat somewhere else,'' Clint said.

"You lead the way, then.''

Clint knew he couldn't take them to Portsmouth Square, not the way they were dressed, but there were plenty of places between the Square and the Coast.

"All right,'' he said, "come on, I think I know a place.''

He took them to a small café a few blocks from the edge of the Barbary Coast where he remembered the food being decent and the coffee being strong.

"This is . . . charming,'' LeConte said.

As they entered they drew attention again, the beauty of the women, the scarlet lining of LeConte's cape.

The place was only half full. They got a table in the back that was large enough to accommodate the five of them. Clint sat across from LeConte, with Gaby on his right and Marie on his left. Jolie sat between Gaby and LeConte, still eyeing Clint with something less than trust.

They ordered steaks on Clint's recommendation, because he figured the kitchen couldn't ruin that.

"Do you have any wine?'' LeConte asked the waiter.

"We don't have no wine here, mister,'' the man answered, "but I could get you a pitcher of beer.''

LeConte looked away, a disappointed expression on his face. Clint looked at Gaby, who nodded.

"Beer will be fine,'' Clint said.

"I did not suspect what a . . . barbarian country this would be.''

"It is not so bad,'' Gaby said.

"When are we going home?" Jolie asked.

"When we finish what we came here to do," Henri LeConte said.

"And what is that?" Clint asked.

LeConte looked at him.

"If I may ask," Clint added.

"And why not?" LeConte asked. "After what you did for us, you are entitled to ask anything."

Clint looked at the three women and wondered if they agreed with that.

EIGHT

"I am sixty years old," LeConte said.

Clint was surprised. He would have guessed the man to be in his forties.

"I have painted all I can paint in France. I decided to come to this country for new vision, new backdrops."

"But the same models?" Clint asked.

LeConte looked around at the three women and smiled.

"I asked my three favorite models to come with me," he said, "and to my delight, they all agreed."

Clint looked at the three women and again wondered which—if any—was warming the artist's bed.

"And you'll paint them?"

"No," LeConte said, "but they will be in every painting I do paint."

"But they won't be the subject?"

"Correct," LeConte said. "They will simply give continuity to my paintings."

"I think I understand," Clint said. "They'll all be re-lated."

"Yes."

Clint looked around at the women.

"What was it that made the three of you agree to leave home and come here?" he asked.

Gaby answered first.

"It is my honor to be one of Henri's models," she said. "I would go anywhere."

He looked at Marie.

"*Oui*, I feel the same," she said.

"And you?" he asked Jolie.

"Me?" she said, with a shrug. "I am crazy."

"I'm surprised that you all speak English so well," Clint said.

"When we all decided to come," Gaby said, "Henri insisted that we all learn the language."

"And you've all learned it so well."

The waiter came with plates up and down his arm just then and laid all five of their meals on the table. Behind him came another waiter with two pitchers of beer and five mugs. Conversation ceased while they made inroads into the contents of their plates. Large steaks and masses of vegetables began to disappear.

When the plates were almost empty LeConte looked across the table at Clint.

"I have a proposition for you, my friend."

"What kind of proposition?"

"Of employment."

Clint poured himself some more beer from the second pitcher.

"You want me to work for you?"

"Yes."

"As what?"

"Well," LeConte said, leaning his elbows on the table, "first, as a model."

"What?" Clint asked, laughing.

"I want to include you in some of my paintings."

"You want to paint me?"

"No," LeConte said, "I want to use you the way I use these lovely young women. You will be part of the painting, not the main subject."

Clint shook his head.

"I don't know . . ."

"Oh, please, Clint," Gaby said, putting her hand on his thigh. "You would be posing with me."

"And with me," Marie said, resting her smaller hand on his other thigh.

"You will pose with all of the girls at one time or another," LeConte said. "Together and individually."

"I don't know about posing—"

"Do not take the fact that we are staying in a lower-class hotel to mean that I do not have money. I can pay you well."

"It's not the money, Mr. LeConte—"

"Please, *mon ami,* call me Henri."

"It's not the money, Henri—"

"It is not only to pose that I wish to hire you," LeConte said quickly.

"There's another reason?"

"Oh yes," LeConte said.

The waiter came at that point to clear the table.

"Will there be anything else?" he asked.

"Some coffee," Clint said.

"Yes, sir. For everyone?"

"For everyone," LeConte said.

"Comin' up."

As the waiter left Clint said, "Okay, Henri, finish your offer."

"I would like to hire you as a guide."

"To where?"

LeConte swept his arm and said, "The West."

"You're in the West, Henri."

"No, I mean the real West—the *wild* West. I want to paint it as it really is, stark, deadly, and I want you to show it to me. The desert, the mountains, the—what are they called—the cow towns?"

Clint thought a moment and while he was thinking he felt Gaby's hand tighten on his thigh. She was a very strong woman.

"Well," he said, "that's, uh, a job I could do more easily—"

"Good, good," LeConte said.

"—but that's not to say that I accept, not yet."

"Why not?"

"Well, I had plans—"

"I think we should give Clint time to think about it," Gaby said suddenly.

"An excellent idea, my dear," LeConte said. "Think over my offer, Clint."

Clint nodded and the waiter came with the coffee. Over coffee Marie and Gaby asked Clint countless questions about what Henri LeConte had called the "old West."

When dinner was over they all stood up and walked

outside, immediately attracting a lot of attention. Outside Gaby took a firmer grip on Clint's left arm.

"I would like to see Portsmouth Square," she said in his ear.

"Neither one of us is dressed for a night on the Square," he said.

"Then perhaps you could just show me your hotel?" she asked.

The way she was looking at him it was hard to deny her, even if she was going to try to seduce him into accepting LeConte's job offer.

"We can find our way back to the hotel," LeConte told Clint. "Why don't you take Gaby for a walk. I am sure she will be safe with you."

"Well," Clint said, "if you're sure you can find your way—"

"I know the way," Jolie said.

"It's not safe to walk around—" Clint started to tell them.

"We will go directly to the hotel," LeConte promised him.

"Well . . . all right, then."

"Good," LeConte said. He looked at Gaby and said, "We will see you later, my dear."

"Shall we go?" Gaby asked Clint.

As Clint and Gaby walked in the opposite direction, Jolie asked Henri LeConte, "Why do we need him?"

"You did not recognize his name?"

"Should I have?"

"If you had done as much research into the American

West as I did, yes."

"Who is he?" Marie asked.

"He is the Gunsmith."

"Who is that?" Jolie asked.

"A legend of the West, my dear," LeConte said, "and I want to get him on my canvas."

NINE

They walked back to Clint's hotel in a leisurely manner. Perhaps they weren't dressed to go into a lot of the hotels in Portsmouth Square, but he was still able to walk her by them.

"They're very lovely," she said. "Perhaps some night we could . . . go inside?"

"I don't see why not," he said. "But you must have some beautiful places like this in France—even *more* beautiful than this."

"Some," she agreed, "but I have not seen those either. You see, in France I am quite poor. That is why I model for Henri."

"Then the prospect of this trip must have been very exciting for you—for all of you."

"Oh, not for all of us," she said.

"Jolie?"

Gaby nodded.

"Why did she come?"

Gaby laughed.

"To stay behind would mean that either Marie or I would be Henri's favorite."

"You compete, the three of you?"

"Jolie competes," Gaby said.

"And Marie?"

"Marie is like a child. She is very happy all the time. Her parents are very rich. She does not pose for the money, as Jolie and I do."

"And you? You don't compete?"

She shrugged.

"I just do not want to be poor."

They continued through the Square and headed for Clint's hotel. The Maxwell was not exactly in the Square, but about a block off of it.

As they entered the lobby no one paid much attention to them. A few men turned and looked at Gaby because she was lovely, but there was not nearly the kind of curiosity she and the others drew on the Barbary Coast.

"All the crystal is lovely," Gaby said, looking around the lobby.

"Would you like me to take you back to your hotel now?" he asked.

She turned and looked at him, a lovely smile, almost mocking, on her face.

"I would rather stay here with you."

"Gaby—"

She put her forefinger on his lips to quiet him.

In his room they undressed each other. Her curves were opulent. She had very large, full breasts with large nipples, wide hips, full thighs, and long legs. She was a big girl all over, with a marvelous, fleshy butt and a real belly. He lost himself in her flesh, licking and sucking her nipples until she whimpered, and then he worked his way down her body, peppering her with kisses until his face was nestled between her legs. His tongue was eager and his cheeks quickly grew wet as he worked her into a frenzy. She started to speak French to him and although he didn't understand her she managed to get her message across. She was grabbing for him and pulled him up on top of her. He entered her sweetly, and she wrapped her strong legs and arms around him. They rocked together until the bed started to move across the floor. She continued to speak French into his ear, but it didn't matter whether he understood her or not. . . .

"What have you decided, Clint?" she asked later.

He was sitting at the foot of the bed. He turned and looked at her. She was sitting with the sheet covering her breasts because she was chilly. He could see the outlines of her nipples against the white sheet.

"I think you look pretty good sitting there," he said.

"You know what I mean," she said. "Will you come to work for Henri?"

"As a guide, maybe."

"And as a model?"

He made a face and said, "I don't think so."

"Why not?"

"It's just not for me."

"Do you think men do not model?"

"I'm sure they do . . . in France."

"But not here?"

"Not in the West, Gaby."

"Afraid of what other men will think?"

"No."

"Then what?"

"Like I said," Clint said, "it's just not for me."

She stared at him for a few moments, then very slowly moved the sheet away from her breasts.

"How about this?" she asked. "Is this for you?"

He got on his hands and knees on the bed and crawled over to her. He kissed her mouth, then her chin, then her neck and finally her breasts. Her nipples puckered beneath his tongue.

"Yes," he said, pulling the sheet away from her completely, "very definitely for me."

TEN

At breakfast, the next morning in the Maxwell dining room, Gaby asked Clint again about the job.

"I would love to see your American West," she said, "and I would love to have you show it to me."

"I told you I'd think about it."

"You had all night to think about it," she said.

He laughed.

"You didn't give me any time to think last night, or don't you remember?"

She laughed, a seductive sound that made the other men in the room turn their heads to look at her.

"I remember very well. I must tell you that Henri intends to drag the three of us out there into the wilderness. Our very lives might depend on you."

"Oh, that's fine," Clint said. "Make me feel guilty."

"I will try anything to get you to take the job."

"Anything?"

She smiled and looked embarrassed.

"No, I did not sleep with you last night to try to get

you to take the job,'' she said, ''but that doesn't mean that I won't . . . tonight.''

Clint laughed and shook his head.

''All right, all right,'' he said, ''I'll take the job.''

''You will model?'' she asked hopefully.

''I will be your guide,'' he said.

''Well,'' she said, ''that will do for a beginning. Come on.''

''Where?'' he asked as she stood up.

''To go and tell Henri. He will be delighted.''

Henri LeConte was not delighted when Clint and Gaby got to the Mystic Palace. When they entered they saw Marie and Jolie in the lobby surrounded by some men, and Marie was crying. One of the men was very large and quite heavy.

''Marie!'' Gaby said.

All eyes turned toward her voice. The men standing around Marie and Jolie looked her up and down, and then turned their attention to Clint.

''Jolie?'' Gaby said. ''What's wrong?''

''It is Henri,'' Jolie said.

''What happened?'' Gaby asked.

''You friends of these girls?'' the large man asked before Jolie could answer.

''Yes, I am,'' Gaby said.

''And you?'' the man asked Clint.

''Yes.''

''What's wrong?'' Gaby asked.

''Do you know a man named Henri LeConte?'' the man asked.

"I know him better than I know you," Clint said.

"My name is Lieutenant Goodman," the man said. "San Francisco Police."

"What's the problem, Lieutenant?"

"Your friend, LeConte?" the lieutenant said. "He's dead."

ELEVEN

"Oh, no," Gaby said, and took Marie into her arms, where the smaller girl sobbed loudly.

"What happened?" Clint asked Goodman.

"First, who are you?"

"My name is Clint Adams."

Lt. Goodman looked around at the other two men who were with him.

"They yours?" Clint asked.

"Sergeant Masters and Officer Pike," Goodman said. "Are you the Gunsmith? That Clint Adams?"

"That's the one."

"What is your connection with these ladies and the dead man?"

"May I take her somewhere?" Gaby asked, still holding Marie.

"She found the body," Jolie told Gaby.

"Oh, God," Gaby said and held Marie tighter.

"Why don't you let the ladies go somewhere and relax," Clint said.

"I'm finished with Miss Deroux and Miss Bouchet,"

Goodman said, reading their names from a piece of paper he'd written them on. Clint assumed he was talking about Marie and Jolie, although he didn't know which was which. It occurred to him then that he didn't know Gaby's last name either.

As if reading his mind, Goodman said to her, "You're Miss Gabrielle Delacroix?"

"That is right."

"Where were you last night?"

"With me," Clint said.

"All night?"

Clint nodded.

"All night."

Goodman looked at Gaby again.

"I'll want to talk to you later. You take care of your friends now."

"Thank you."

Gaby put one arm out to gather Jolie in, and the three women walked off together.

"Mr. Adams," Goodman said, "can we talk?"

"Sure."

Goodman looked at his men and something passed between them. They both nodded and moved off.

"How about a cup of coffee?" Goodman asked.

"Sure, if you're buying."

Goodman smiled for the first time.

"I'm buying."

"Let's go."

When they had a table and a cup of coffee each, Goodman explained what had apparently happened to Henri LeConte.

"Somebody got into his room and slit his throat," the policeman said. "The little gal . . . uh, Marie?"

"Right."

"She found·him in the morning."

"Anybody see anyone?"

"Not that we know of. I have men asking around in the area. When did you last see Mr. LeConte?"

"Last night."

"What time?"

"I don't really remember. After dinner. About nine, I guess."

"And Miss Delacroix went with you?"

"Yes."

"He and the other women went off together?"

"Yes."

"Back here?"

"As far as I know."

"How well do you know them?"

"We met yesterday."

"And Miss Delacroix went back to your hotel with you last night?"

"Yes."

"Is she . . ."

"No," Clint said, "she is not a whore."

"And the others?"

"Not them either," Clint said.

"The other two say they're models and the dead man was an artist."

"That's what they all told me. In fact, I saw him painting them."

"When?"

Clint told Goodman what had transpired on the docks the day before.

"Four men, you say?"

"That's right."

"Describe them."

Clint did so and Goodman listened intently.

"The older one," he said when Clint was finished, "his name is John."

"Just John?"

"Nobody knows his first name. He's the dangerous one."

"That was the impression I got."

"He goes around with one called Bell."

"Bell introduced himself. Why does John bother with him?" Clint asked.

Goodman shrugged.

"I wonder the same thing."

"Is Bell the brains?"

"No smarter than John. Sometimes I think that John just doesn't want to bother with thinking, you know?"

"How do you know them?" Clint asked.

"They're in and out of San Francisco," Goodman said. "At least, John and Bell are."

"And the other two?"

"There are usually four, and the other two vary," Goodman said.

"You think they did this?" Clint asked.

"I don't know," the lieutenant said. "Anybody could have done it, right now."

"The girls?"

"Maybe. I'll have to talk with Miss Delacroix."

"You can, but she was with me."

"Maybe she can tell me about the other two."

"What about them?"

"Well, for one thing, which one was sleeping with the artist."

"She would have to tell you that," Clint confirmed. "I don't know the pecking order."

"Maybe all of them," Goodman said. "Maybe one of them got jealous."

"Maybe."

Goodman studied Clint for a few moments.

"You're right, that's *my* job. Look, since you're apparently involved with them I'd like it if none of you left San Francisco until I solved this."

"I wasn't planning to leave, just yet."

"Well, now that the artist is dead, the ladies might take it into their heads to go back home to their own country. I can't have that. Not until I've solved this thing."

"There's no reason for them to listen to me," Clint said. "You better tell them."

"I will. I'll tell Miss Delacroix."

"Where's the body?" Clint asked.

"It hasn't been removed yet," Goodman said, "but it will be soon."

"How were they set up? In rooms, I mean."

"I don't know," Goodman said. "I mean, there are two rooms, but I don't know what the sleeping arrangements were."

"Well, they're all probably in the other room," Clint said. "How about if I go up and stay with Marie and Jolie, and send Gabrielle down here to talk to you?"

Goodman nodded and said, "All right. I'll wait here for her. Thanks."

"No problem," Clint said, standing up. "Thanks for the coffee."

"Adams?"

Clint turned.

"Are you gonna get involved in this?"

"Like you said, Lieutenant," Clint replied, "I already am."

TWELVE

When Clint knocked, the door was opened by Gaby.

"The lieutenant wants to talk to you."

He turned and looked at Marie and Jolie. The blonde was lying down, while the black girl was sitting on the bed next to her.

"I'll stay with them," he said.

She looked at him.

"What should I tell him?"

"Tell him the truth. You have nothing to hide, do you?" he asked.

"Well . . . no, I do not. None of us do."

"Then go and talk to the man. I'll stay here with them."

Gaby took one more look at the other two women.

"All right." She turned and said, "I'll be right back. Clint will stay with you."

She walked past Clint, who touched her briefly as she went by, then stepped inside and closed the door.

He stared at Marie and Jolie for a long moment before he realized that Marie was asleep.

"She cried herself to sleep."

"What happened, Jolie?"

She looked up at him and said, "Somebody killed Henri."

"Who?"

"I don't know."

"Why was it Marie who found his body?"

Jolie didn't answer.

"Didn't the police ask you that question?"

"Yes."

"What did you tell them?"

"That she went to wake him up."

"Was that the truth?"

Jolie hesitated, then said, "No."

"Then what is the truth?"

"She . . . went to be with him."

"To join him in his bed?"

"Yes."

"Why?"

"She always did, in the morning."

"And what about the rest of the night?"

"Sometimes one of us stayed with him awhile, but he slept alone. He could not sleep with someone else in the bed."

"So you were with him last night?"

"Yes."

"How long?"

"Not long."

"Then he spent most of the night alone?"

"Yes."

"Why didn't you tell the police?"

She sneered.

"I can tell by the looks on their faces they think we are whores."

He couldn't tell her she was wrong.

"All right. Did you hear anything during the night?"

"No."

"When Marie went to wake him up, was the door unlocked?" he asked.

Jolie looked at the sleeping blonde.

"You will have to ask her . . . but don't wake her now."

"I won't," he said. "I'll ask her later."

She looked at Clint again.

"What do we do now?"

Clint moved to the end of the bed but did not sit on it. He didn't want to wake Marie.

"The lieutenant is explaining it to Gaby now," he said. "He doesn't want you to leave San Francisco."

"We could not go home even if we wanted to," she said.

"Why not?"

"We have no money."

"I thought—Henri told me he had plenty of money," Clint said.

"He did," she said, "but we have none."

"No money of your own?"

She shook her head.

"Henri paid for everything," she said.

"Didn't he pay you girls?"

"No."

"Didn't he give you any money?"

"No," she said. "He paid for everything, but he never gave us money. So you see, we can't afford to go back home. We can't even afford to stay in this hotel."

"There must be some money in his room," Clint said.

"I don't know. He never told us where he kept it."

"After they move his body," Clint said, "we'll look around."

"What are we going to do now?" she asked again.

"Just try to relax, Jolie," Clint said. "We'll figure something out."

"Why?"

"What do you mean, why?"

"Why are you going to help us?"

She was looking at him funny, like he was a kind of man she had never come across before.

"Somebody has to help you," he said.

"But why you?"

"Is there anybody else you know in this country?" he asked.

"No," she said, looking away. "There's just the three of us."

"Then I'm all you've got."

THIRTEEN

Clint was looking out the window when Gaby returned to the room twenty minutes later. Marie was still asleep and Jolie was still sitting by her. As Gaby entered the room, Marie woke up.

"Is it over?" she asked, sitting up.

"It is not going to be over until the police find out who killed Henri," Gaby said.

"What did they ask you?" Jolie asked.

"The same things they asked you, I am sure."

"They think we are whores."

"Yes," Gaby said, "they do."

"But . . . why?" Marie asked.

"That is the way they think," Gaby said.

"Have they removed . . . the body, Gaby?"

"I saw some men come in and come upstairs," she said. "I did not see them leave."

"Where was Henri's room?" Clint asked.

"At the end of the hall," Jolie said.

"Don't make me go back there," Marie said.

Gaby went and sat next to her, on the opposite side of the bed from Jolie.

"No one is going to force you, Marie," she said, comforting the woman.

"Stay here," Clint said. "I'll be back after they've removed . . . Henri."

"We will stay here."

As Clint went out the door he heard Gaby explaining to the others how the lieutenant had told her they were not to leave the country.

When he reached Henri's room the door was open and some men were lifting him from the bed. Lieutenant Goodman was standing off to one side, watching. Clint had to step aside to let the men carry Henri's body out of the room.

"What are you looking for, Adams?" Goodman asked.

"I was wondering about LeConte's things. His paints, brushes, personal belongings."

"What about them? You want them?"

"Not me," Clint said. "The . . . the ladies."

"Oh," Goodman said, "the . . . ladies. Well, are any of them married to him?"

"No."

"Then I guess they're not entitled to his belongings, are they?"

"Maybe not," Clint said, "but they haven't got much else. What do you say?"

Goodman stared at him for a moment, then walked to the door.

"Okay," he said finally, "they can go in and take them. I don't need them."

"Thanks, Lieutenant."

The man nodded and stepped past Clint into the hallway.

"Tell me something," Clint said.

"What?"

"How do you figure the killer got in?"

"Well," Goodman said, "the window was locked, and when the little blond woman came to wake him up she said the door was unlocked. I guess the killer got in through the door."

"So it was either open," Clint said, "or Henri LeConte let his killer in."

"Which would mean he knew the killer."

"Right."

"And how many people in America did Mr. LeConte know?" Goodman asked.

"Well . . . the girls, and . . ."

"And you, Adams," Goodman said, patting Clint on the shoulder. "Remember what I said. Don't leave town—or the country."

FOURTEEN

Clint went back down the hall to the room the women were in.

"The police are gone," he told them, "and we have permission to go into the room."

"For what?" Gaby asked.

"I don't want to go into the room," Marie said, sobbing.

"Don't whine, dear," Jolie said.

Gaby was still looking at Clint.

"Jolie says you girls have no money of your own," Clint said.

"That is true."

"Then we should go into Henri's room and see if he left any there."

"Take money from a . . . dead man?" Gaby asked, looking shocked.

"Gaby," Clint said, "do you want to go back home, to France?"

"Well, yes, but—"

"Tickets cost money, and Henri isn't here to take care of it for you this time."

Gaby started to say something, then stopped and thought a moment.

"You are right, of course," she said. She looked at the other women and then back to Clint. "I will go."

"I'll go with you."

"Thank you," she said, with feeling.

"We'll be right back," Clint said to Marie and Jolie.

"We have nowhere to go," Jolie said.

Clint and Gaby started down the hall.

"What's Jolie's story?" he asked.

"Her story? I don't understand."

"Why is she so distrustful of men?"

"Oh," Gaby said, "you noticed that. It is true, she does not trust many men. Things happened to her in her youth that leave her unable to trust."

"Did she trust Henri?"

"Completely."

"Jolie indicated that you girls, uh, took turns sleeping with him."

"She and Marie did," Gaby said.

"Not you?"

"No."

"Why not?"

"I have been—had been—with Henri the longest. I made it clear a long time ago that I would model for him, but I would not have sex with him."

Clint took a good look at Gaby, a hard look, and decided she was telling him the truth.

"You don't believe me?" Gaby asked.

"Uh, no—I mean, yes, I do believe you."

"Why are you staring at me?"

"Because even with everything that has happened I still can't help admiring how beautiful you are."

"Ah, Clint Adams," she said, "you are a dangerous man, I think."

They reached LeConte's room and Gaby stopped short of going in.

"Just give me a minute, please?"

"Of course," he said, patting her arm. "I'll go in and start looking around. Why don't you come in when you're ready?"

"All right."

Clint left her in the hall and went into the room to take a look around. LeConte had unpacked his clothes and put them in the chest of drawers. Clint found quite a few silk shirts and fancy pants, but he didn't find any money in any of the clothing.

There was a closet in the room, which he checked. Again, LeConte had some fancy jackets and greatcoats hanging there, but when Clint went through the pockets he found no money.

"Have you found anything?" Gaby asked.

Clint turned and saw that she was staring at the bloody sheets on the bed as she spoke to him. Clint wished that Goodman would have removed them.

He walked to Gaby and took her by the shoulders. She jerked her eyes from the bed and looked at him.

"I haven't found anything, Gaby. You said you were with Henri the longest. Where would he hide his money?"

"I did not even think he was hiding money."

"Well, it's not around here . . . unless . . ."

"Unless what?"

Now he looked at the bloody sheets.

"Unless he hid it under the mattress."

She closed her eyes and said, "*Merde.* . . . "

Clint didn't ask her what it meant. He had a feeling he already knew.

FIFTEEN

Once again Gaby went out of the room to wait in the hall while Clint lifted the bloody mattress and felt around underneath it.

Nothing.

Clint stood in the center of the room and looked around for a likely hiding place. He walked around the room once, looking for loose floorboards.

"Nothing," Clint reported to Gaby in the hall.

"What about the policemen?" she asked.

"What about them?"

"Couldn't they have taken the money?"

"I guess they could have, but there are other possibilities, as well."

"Like what?"

"Well, maybe he left it at the desk, to be put in the hotel safe—if this hotel has a safe."

"We must check."

"All right. Let's go downstairs now and ask," Clint said.

They walked past the room where Jolie and Marie were

62

and went down the stairs to talk to the desk clerk.

"This is terrible," the man said, mopping his face with a handkerchief. "Nobody's ever been killed in this hotel before."

"Did Mr. LeConte leave anything with you for safe-keeping?" Clint asked.

"Who?" The clerk stared at him from behind thick eyeglasses.

"The dead man."

"Oh, the French fellow," the clerk said.

"Yes, did he leave anything for you to put into the hotel safe?"

"We don't have a hotel safe."

"Well, did he leave anything with you, anyway?" Clint asked, growing annoyed.

"No, why should he?"

Clint wondered about the clerk, whether the man would have the nerve to steal from a dead man. He didn't think so.

"All right, thanks," Clint said. He turned to Gaby and said, "We better get back to the others."

He walked with her back upstairs and into the second hotel room.

"Did you find anything?" Jolie asked.

"No," Gaby said, "nothing."

"Think, Gaby," Clint said. "Where would Henri hide his money?"

"Where?" she asked. "I don't even know why he would hide it from us. Did he think we would steal it?"

"He may not have hidden it from you," Clint said. "Maybe he just didn't trust the people in this country.

After what happened yesterday, he probably had good cause to be distrustful.''

"Yes," Gaby said, "what about those men? Could they be the killers?"

"It's possible," Clint said. "I told the police about them and they're going to look for them."

"I will bet it was them, those pigs," Marie said.

"Who else could it have been?" Jolie asked.

The question hung in the air for a few moments while they all exchanged glances.

"Clint?" Gaby asked. "Who else could they think it was?"

"They think it was somebody he knew."

"But he knew only us, in this country," she said.

"And you," Jolie said to him. He wondered if she was accusing him.

"Clint was with me all night," Gaby said, "so it could not have been him, or me."

"Are you saying it was one of us?" Jolie asked.

"Gaby!" Marie said, in horror.

"I am not saying that," Gaby said. "I know it was none of us. What we have to find out is who *did* do it so we can go home."

"And how will we do that?" Jolie asked. "We are not detectives."

Gaby turned and looked at Clint.

"Will you help us?" she asked.

"I'm not a detective either," he said, "but I'll do what I can."

"Thank you, Clint," Marie said.

"You all have to understand something," he said. "I'm

also doing this to help myself. I'm under suspicion, and I can't leave San Francisco either until Henri's killer is found."

"Good," Jolie said. "When you find him you kill him."

"I'm not a killer."

"But . . ." Jolie said, and let it trail off.

"But what?" he asked. "Come on."

"Henri said you were . . . a legend in the American West. He said you had killed many men."

"Is this true?" Gaby asked. Obviously, Henri had talked to Jolie and Marie while Gaby was with Clint.

"I've killed men who were trying to kill me," Clint said.

"But . . . are you a legend?" Gaby asked.

"That's not a question I can answer comfortably."

"Henri said you were called the Gunsmith," Marie said.

"That's true."

"But . . . I have heard of you," Gaby said. "I did not connect your name with . . . with that name."

"Then you *will* be able to help us," Marie said.

"I said I would try," Clint said, "but I'll be doing it for all of us. Is that acceptable?"

"As long as it gets done," Gaby said.

"Then you ladies are going to have to be very frank with me."

"What is 'frank'?" Marie asked.

"Honest," Gaby said. "Clint wants us to be honest with him."

"That is funny," Jolie said.

"What is?" Clint asked.

"A man asking us to trust him."

"Do you find it very hard to trust men, Jolie?" Clint asked.

"Impossible."

"But you trusted Henri?"

"I understood Henri," she said. "I knew what he wanted from me."

"And what was that?"

"He wanted me to model, and he wanted sex."

"And that was all right with you?"

"Yes," she said. "I just want to know what a man expects of me."

"Well, right now," Clint said, "all I expect is for you to answer all my questions as truthfully as you can. All right?"

"Yes," she said. "All right."

"Good."

SIXTEEN

For the next hour Clint questioned all three girls. He concentrated on who they might have met during their trip, starting with the ship they came in on.

"There was some trouble on the ship," Gaby admitted.

"What kind of trouble?"

Gaby looked at Marie.

"Marie became . . . friends with a man on the ship," she said.

"He was a boy," Marie argued, "a sweet boy."

"Perhaps," Gaby said, "but his friends were not so sweet."

"He would not have done it if they had not forced him."

"What happened?" Clint asked.

"They were pigs," Jolie said, "and so was your sweet boy."

Clint had to take Jolie's opinion with a grain of salt. After all, she thought all men were pigs.

"What happened?" he asked again.

"That sweet boy lured Marie down to his bed, or bunk, whatever they call it."

"His friends were waiting there," Jolie said. "They were all going to have her."

"And?"

"Henri stopped them," Gaby said. "He knew what the crew was thinking. We went looking for Marie and when we found her they had her naked on one of the beds."

"Her 'sweet boy' was going to be first," Jolie said with contempt.

Clint thought about Marie naked on a bed in a room full of men.

"And Henri was able to stop them?"

"We brought the captain with us," Gaby said.

"And then what happened?"

"Nothing," Jolie said. "No one was punished."

"We took Marie away with us, and the captain told us to stay inside for the rest of the trip."

"He said it was our own fault," Jolie said. "He said we were asking for it. Just like a man."

"Did you see any of the crew after you got off?" Clint asked.

"No."

"Did any of them threaten you?"

"Not out loud," Gaby said.

"What does that mean?"

"Well . . . we got a lot of dirty looks as we got off the ship."

Disappointed men, no doubt, Clint thought. When the crew saw the three women get on in France there must have been quite a reaction. For the women to have gotten off ''untouched'' must have been very disappointing for some of the men.

''But no one said anything?''

''No.''

''Or followed you?''

Gaby frowned.

''Not that we know of.''

''If it was one of the crew,'' Marie said, ''why would they kill Henri and not come after . . . us?''

It was a good question. Clint thought it more likely that men from the ship would follow and try to grab one of the girls—probably Marie—and finish what they'd started on the ship.

''I don't know,'' Clint said. ''Maybe somebody lost his job over what happened?''

''I doubt that,'' Jolie said.

''Why?''

''Because the captain was looking at us the same way his men were.''

Clint looked at Gaby.

''It's true,'' she said. ''When we found them with Marie I think he was more angry because nobody had told him what was going on so he could be there.''

Clint got off the subject of the ship then and started asking if they'd had trouble with anyone else other than Bell and John and the other two men.

''We have been looked at by a lot of men,'' Gaby said, ''but no one approached us until they did.''

''I think you will find most men in the West respectful of women,'' Clint said.

Jolie made a rude sound and looked away.

"Clint, what do we do now?" Marie asked.

"Well," Clint said, "first we'll have to get you girls another hotel room. You can't all three sleep in here."

"We can't afford this room, let alone another one," Gaby said.

"Well—"

"But you already have another room, don't you?" she went on, not giving him a chance to say anything.

"Well—" he said again.

"One of us should stay with you while the other two stay here," she finished.

He eyed her, wondering which one of them she had in mind to stay with him.

"I will stay with Marie," Jolie said.

Clint thought Marie looked a little disappointed—or was he just stroking his own ego?

"Well," Gaby said, smiling at him with her back to the other women, "I guess that means I'll be staying with you until this is all over."

"I guess."

SEVENTEEN

Clint left the three women alone in the room and exited the hotel. He didn't intend to leave them alone for long. It occurred to him that now that Henri had been killed, they might also be in danger. He needed to get them some protection.

The first place he thought of for that was the police. Since Goodman and all his men were gone, he'd have to go to Goodman's office to talk to him.

The Barbary Coast was Goodman's responsibility, so the police station was located not far from the hotel. When Clint got there he presented himself at the front desk and asked for Lieutenant Goodman.

"Who wants him?" the policeman behind the desk asked.

"Clint Adams."

"What's it about?"

"It's about the murder of Henri LeConte."

"Henri . . . who?" the man asked.

"Just tell him it's about the murder earlier today," Clint said. "He'll know."

The policeman gave the message to another man to deliver.

"Just have a seat," he told Clint.

There was a bench against a wall and Clint went over and sat. He was there only a few moments when Goodman lumbered in and stood before him.

"Are you here to confess, Adams?"

"No, I'm afraid it's not going to be that easy."

"Then you're probably here to poke your nose into my business."

"I'm here to—"

Goodman raised his hand and said, "Save it until we're in my office. Follow me."

The lieutenant turned and walked back the way he had come, with Clint following. He never once looked back to see if Clint was still with him.

When they reached his office, Goodman circled his desk and sat down. He didn't invite Clint to sit, but since he had invited him into his office Clint assumed that this would be permissible. He sat.

"What is it?" Goodman asked.

"I think the women are going to need protection the rest of the time they're here."

"Why?"

"Well, it's possible that whoever killed LeConte might come after them, isn't it?"

"Unless one of them killed him."

"You don't really believe that, do you?"

"No," Goodman said, "I don't have any reason to believe it . . . but I don't have any reason not to believe it either."

"Hey, Gabrielle was with me."

"Which means that you two could have done it to-gether," Goodman pointed out, "or the other two could have done it. Or either one of them."

"Or someone else."

Goodman gave Clint a tired smile.

"Right now I'm working on the assumption that any-one could have done it."

"Fine, then we're back where we started. I think the women need protection."

"Then protect them."

"I can't."

"Why not?"

"I'm . . ."

"Gonna be poking your nose in my business?" Good-man asked. "Are you gonna play detective on me, Ad-ams? That's all I need, you know. You getting in the way."

"I'm not going to get in the way."

"Yes, you are. I know your type, Adams. Can't sit back and let the police do their job. You've gotta try to help, right?"

"I'm not trying to help you," Clint said. "I'm trying to help me, and those women."

"How's that?"

"We can't leave San Francisco until you find the kill-ers."

"So why not sit back and wait? Enjoy what the city has to offer?"

"Because—"

"Because you can't, can you?" Goodman said, without

giving Clint a chance to answer. "Because waiting is not in your blood, is it? You're a man of action. That's how you got your reputation."

"You don't know the first thing about me, Lieutenant," Clint said.

"I think I do."

Clint stood up.

"Are you going to give those women some protection or not?"

"I don't have the manpower to have someone stay with them twenty-four hours . . . as nice as that job might sound. No, if you want those women protected I'm afraid you're gonna have to see to it yourself."

Goodman was smart. He knew that if Clint couldn't leave the women alone, then he wouldn't be poking around.

"Thanks for your help, Lieutenant."

"Glad to oblige."

Clint left the office and the building, his mind already racing, searching his memory, trying to find someone he knew and could trust in San Francisco.

EIGHTEEN

Clint had known a couple of detectives in San Francisco at one time, but they had both pulled up stakes and moved to Sacramento. Why, he didn't know. Maybe he'd find out sometime in the future.

There was another man he knew, but they weren't particularly friends. He knew the man hired out for different kinds of jobs, including bodyguard. He also knew the man was expensive. He decided to get in touch and see if he was available.

Able Tracker lived in a hotel just outside of Portsmouth Square. Some people said he'd won the hotel in a poker game, but for one reason or another the owner of record was a man named Duke Farrell. It was known that Farrell often fronted for Tracker.

Clint entered the hotel and went to the front desk. The place was just a step—maybe even a half a step—down from the fine, fancy hotels in the Square.

"Can I help you, sir?" the lady behind the desk asked. She was a stunning woman with a mass of red hair cascading down over her shoulders.

"Yes, I'd like to see Mr. Farrell, please."

"Would you like a room, sir?" she asked.

Sure, he thought, with you.

"No, thank you, I just need to see Mr. Farrell."

"Can I tell him what it's about, sir?" Clint detected an Irish accent, which made sense given the pale skin and red hair.

"I think I'll tell him that."

"Fine," she said, with a smile. "And your name?"

"Clint Adams."

If she recognized it—and was impressed—she hid it well.

"Why don't you go in and have some coffee, sir, and I'll tell Duke you're here."

"And what's your name?"

"Shana, sir."

"Thank you, Shana."

He turned and went into the dining room. By the time he was seated and had a pot of coffee in front of him, Duke Farrell appeared in the doorway.

Farrell was a diminutive man, standing only about five foot five. He was a gambler by trade, and his friendship with Able Tracker was a strange one. Nobody knew its roots—no one but them, of course. The two men were not alike, and yet they fit together so well.

Farrell walked across the room and stared down at Clint. The only time he was able to stare down at anyone was when the person was seated and he was standing.

"Hello, Clint."

"How are you, Duke?"

"I'm fine," Farrell said. "I'm a little surprised to see

you here. Shana said you didn't want a room."

"No, I don't," Clint said. "Why don't you have a seat, Duke, and help me with this coffee. Is it good coffee?"

Farrell sat opposite him. He was impeccably dressed in a dark suit and a boiled white shirt.

"If I remember correctly, you like your coffee strong and black."

"Right."

"Then you should like this."

Clint poured two cups and tasted his.

"You're right," he said truthfully. "It's good."

Farrell sipped some and put the cup down. He never picked it up again.

"What can I do for you?"

"I have a problem and I need some help."

"From me?"

"You and Tracker. Is he in town?"

"Why don't you tell me what your problem is first," Farrell suggested.

Briefly Clint told him about meeting Henri LeConte and his three models, about the altercation on the docks, and then about the murder.

"And you're afraid the women might be in danger now?" Farrell asked when he was finished.

"I think it's a possibility."

Farrell thought a moment.

"Tracker's not in San Francisco, Clint," he told him. "But I think I know a man who could help you."

"Is he good?"

"He's very good," Farrell said. "He's not Tracker,

mind you, but he's good.''

"Can you put me in touch with him?''

"I'll have him come to your hotel,'' Farrell said. "Where are you staying?''

"The Maxwell.''

"Good new hotel.''

"Will he take the job? I mean, how can you be sure he'll come to my hotel?''

"He'll take the job,'' Farrell said. "Don't worry. He'll be at your hotel later today. I don't know what time, but it shouldn't be more than a few hours from now.''

"What's his name?'' Clint asked.

"Ryker.''

"Ryker . . . what?''

"Just Ryker.''

"What's he look like?''

"He's thirty. A little young, maybe, but he's good. He's about five nine, dark-haired, real good-looking to the ladies.''

"Ryker.''

"Right. Go back to your hotel and wait. He'll be there.''

Clint frowned.

"I recommend him highly, Clint. I know you may not want to use somebody you don't know, but I recommend him highly. Tracker would, too, if he was here.''

"I'll have to take your word for that.''

"Look,'' Farrell said, "talk to him and if you don't like him you don't have to use him . . . but you do need somebody, right?''

"Right.''

Clint stood up and said, "Thanks for the coffee."

"You let me know how it works out."

"Don't worry," Clint said, "you'll be the first to know if it doesn't."

"By the way," Farrell said.

"What?"

"Somebody's following you."

"How do you know?"

Farrell shrugged.

"Who is it?"

"Fella called Sammy Jenks."

"Sammy?" Clint asked. "Works for a man named Garland?"

"That's right. You know Garland?"

"He's a friend of a friend. Why would he have somebody following me?"

"Maybe he's just keeping an eye on you," Farrell said, "since you're a friend of a friend."

"Maybe . . ." Clint said.

"What are you gonna do?"

"Nothing, right now," Clint said. "Thanks for letting me know."

"You would have noticed sooner or later," Farrell said.

"Yeah."

"You would have noticed by now if you didn't have so much on your mind."

"Sure."

"That's why you need Ryker."

"I'll talk to him, Duke."

"Fine, fine."

"I'll see you."

"Sure."

Clint walked through the lobby, took one more look at the redhead behind the desk—she smiled at him—and then went out the door. He headed back to his own hotel to wait for Farrell's man, Ryker.

After Clint left the hotel Farrell approached Shana at the desk.

"Was that really him?" she asked. "The Gunsmith?"

"It really was."

"Why was he looking for you? Are you friends?"

"Acquaintances," Farrell said. "And he wasn't looking for me, he was looking for Tracker."

"But Tracker's not in San Francisco."

"I know," Farrell said, "that's what I told him."

"Are he and Tracker friends?"

"No."

"Is he—"

"Shana, have you seen Ryker?"

He knew if he didn't cut her off, she'd keep asking questions.

"Not today."

"See if someone can find him, will you? I've got to talk to him."

"All right." She looked past him at the doorway and said, "So that was really him, huh?"

"Yes, Shana," Farrell said, "that was really him." He leaned on the desk and said softly, "Find me Ryker, hmm?"

She pulled her eyes from the doorway and looked at him.

"Right away."

NINETEEN

Now that he knew Sammy was there Clint spotted him instantly. He realized why he hadn't seen him earlier. The man was very good at what he was doing.

On the way back to his hotel Clint decided that it was not safe to leave the women at their Barbary Coast hotel—not even if they had Ryker guarding them. The best thing for them would be to move them to another hotel—preferably one closer to his, but not as expensive. The cost was a factor since he'd be footing the bill unless they could find out where Henri LeConte was hiding his money.

Instead of going back to the Maxwell, he went to get the French women, with Sammy Jenks in tow.

"We don't have time to argue," Clint said to the three women. "Until I can get you protection I have to keep you with me. Just pack your things and let's go."

"All right," Gaby said. She turned and spoke to Marie and Jolie in French. After that they all started to pack, with Jolie casting suspicious looks Clint's way the entire time.

Clint walked to the window and looked out. Sammy Jenks seemed as good at hiding himself as he did at following someone. He couldn't see him anywhere.

"What is it?" Gaby asked.

"Someone is following me."

"The killer?"

"I don't think so. I don't think it's connected to the killing."

"Then who is it?"

"I know who it is," he said. "I just don't know why."

"How will you find out?"

He looked at her and said, "I'll have to ask, but I'll do it later. Right now I've got to get you three to my hotel. I've got to meet someone there."

"Who?"

"A man who is going to watch you."

"And what are you going to do?"

"I'm going to try to find out who killed Henri."

"That will be dangerous."

"It might."

"But you are used to danger, are you not?"

"I've been in danger before, yes."

"Then you know how to be careful, no?"

He smiled and said, "I know how to be careful, yes."

She smiled, too, and said, "That is very good."

"Are we ready, ladies?" he asked loudly.

"We are ready," Marie said.

Jolie didn't answer, but she had her bag in hand. Clint was surprised that three beautiful women had been able to travel so light, and he commented on it.

"The clothing we used to model in is in Henri's room," Gaby said.

"We won't be needing it, then," he said.

"We are going to leave all those clothes behind?" Marie asked, sounding as if she was about to burst into tears.

"We have to travel light, Marie." He looked at Gaby and said, "I'll go down and find a cab. Watch from the window and don't come down until you see me wave. Okay?"

"All right."

He started for the door and stopped when she called his name.

"Yes?"

She moved close to him and asked, "Do you really think we are in danger?"

"I don't know anything for certain, Gaby," he said, "but I'd rather play it safe."

"You are very kind to help us when you have only known us a short time," she said.

"Let's put it this way," he said. "Other than each other, I'm the oldest friend you have in this country."

She widened her eyes and added, "And the only one."

TWENTY

When Clint got to the Maxwell he had to talk to the manager in order to get two more rooms. He had decided they'd be safest in the same hotel as him. As long as it was only a couple of night, he could afford to pay for their accommodations. That was, if he could persuade the manager.

"It's impossible, Mr. Adams," the man said. He was in his forties, with a carefully trimmed, pencil-thin mustache and greased down black hair. "We're very busy—"

"Look over there," Clint said, pointing across the lobby to where the three women stood. "Have you ever seen three such beautiful women in one place at one time?"

"Well . . . no, as a matter of fact, I haven't—"

"Those women are looking for a hero, Mr. . . . ?"

"Morgan," the man said, "my name is Morgan."

"The man they came here with from France was brutally murdered, Mr. Morgan," Clint said, "and these three lovely ladies are looking for a hero."

"A hero?"

"Someone who will help them in their time of need."

"Well . . . what is it they need?"

"They need rooms, Mr. Morgan, just for a few days while the police catch the people who killed their . . . benefactor. They need a place to be safe, where they can sleep peacefully and not be afraid. Is this that place, Mr. Morgan? Are you that hero?"

Morgan looked across the lobby at the three women again. Gaby must have had some idea what was going on because she tossed the manger a smoldering look across the floor.

"Well . . . I suppose a couple of rooms for a couple of days wouldn't hurt," Morgan said finally.

"I knew these ladies could count on you, Mr. Morgan. Would you be so kind as to put the rooms in my name? I'll be paying."

"Of course, Mr. Adams. Would the ladies like assistance in taking their bags up?"

"I don't think so," Clint said. "I think we can manage. If you'll just get the keys?"

"Oh, surely."

While the manager went to get the room keys Clint went to stand with the women.

"What did you promise him?" Gaby asked.

"Just that he would be a hero," Clint said. "When he comes over with the keys, try to treat him like one. Okay?"

"Of course," Gaby said.

"Hmph," Jolie said.

"All right," Marie said.

Clint was worried about Jolie, but even she gave Morgan a bright smile when he brought them their keys and assured them that they would not be bothered as long as they were staying in *his* hotel.

All three women thanked him profusely and stroked his cheek. They left the hotel manager standing in the middle of the lobby with a red face.

"You girls were great," Clint said.

"We know how to make a man feel special," Jolie said. "So many of them need that—even when they aren't."

"Ignore her," Gaby said to Clint. "She is always in a bad humor."

"I am not," Jolie said.

"Yes, you are," Marie said, "and almost always when there are men around. I honestly don't know why you don't like men, Jolie."

"And you probably never will, Marie," Jolie said. "I am happy for you."

Upstairs on the second floor they found their two rooms down the hall from Clint's.

"Two rooms?" Gaby asked, giving Clint a look.

"Well," he said, with a shrug, "he happened to have two available."

"Now one of us won't have to share Clint's room," Marie said, nudging Jolie who—for a change—smiled a genuine smile at Gaby's expense.

"Get settled in, ladies," Clint said. "I have to go downstairs and meet someone."

"Our bodyguard?" Marie asked.

"Yes."

"Will he be handsome?"

"He will be very handsome, Marie."

"Oh, good."

"Marie," Jolie said, putting her arm around her friend, "you and I really have to talk."

TWENTY-ONE

Clint went back downstairs, wondering if Ryker had been by looking for him yet. He glanced around the lobby quickly but saw no one who fit Duke Farrell's description. He walked to the desk and asked the clerk if anyone had asked for him.

"Sorry, sir, no one."

"Well, if anyone does I'll be in the hotel bar."

"Yes, sir."

He crossed the lobby and entered the hotel bar, which at this time of the day was not doing a very brisk business, which suited him fine.

He wondered what Sammy Jenks was thinking, wherever he was hiding himself. He had come to the conclusion that Jenks had to be following him at Eddie Garland's order. What he wanted to find out was why. As soon as he was freed up from guarding the women, he'd go to Garland and find out. While he was hunting for a murderer he didn't need to be looking over his shoulder all the time.

Of course, that wouldn't happen unless he was satisfied that Ryker could do the job.

He got himself a beer and took it to a corner table from where he'd be able to watch both entrances to the place. He was halfway through it when a man entered from the hotel lobby. He fit the description. Clint studied the man while the man studied the room. For a man who was so highly thought of by Duke Farrell, Ryker was remarkably devoid of any sort of arrogant demeanor.

Clint waited until Ryker looked the whole room over. He was sure that the man had spotted him long before, and he liked the thoroughness with which he surveyed the room before walking over to his table.

"Mr. Adams?"

"That's right." An arrogant man would just have said, "Adams?"

"I'm Ryker."

"Sit down—or get yourself a beer first."

"That's okay," Ryker said, sitting opposite him. "I don't need one."

"Suit yourself."

"Duke Farrell said you might have a job for me."

"I might."

"What kind?"

"Bodyguard."

"For whom?"

"Three women."

Ryker looked pensive. Clint could see why Farrell had said he was attractive to women. He wasn't handsome, but he was pleasant-looking. Clint wondered if smiling would *make* him handsome.

"It's hard enough to guard one person," Ryker said, rubbing his jaw, "but three?"

"I'm footing the bill on this, Ryker," Clint said, "so I can't tell you that there's a lot of money in it. Truth is, I was going to try to convince Tracker to do it for me as a favor."

"Done."

"What?"

"I'll do it as a favor."

"I can't ask you to do that."

"You haven't even asked me to do the job yet, Mr. Adams, but if you do, I'll do it as a favor."

"Why?"

"Because you know Duke, and you know Tracker, and ... since we're being truthful, I'd be interested in working with you."

"I'd have to pay you something," Clint insisted.

Ryker shrugged and said, "Pay me whatever is fair."

"I should give you some background, as well." Clint said. "Maybe you won't want to take the job."

"All right," Ryker said, and Clint told him the story, everything that had happened since he first met Henri LeConte and the three models. He even told him about Eddie Garland and Sammy Jenks.

"I know Sammy," Ryker said when Clint was finished. "He's no danger to you. He most likely is just keeping an eye on you."

"Well, I intend to talk to Garland about it. What do you know about him?"

"He's a good friend to have, and a bad enemy."

"Which is he to you?"

"Neither," Ryker said. "I haven't had any dealings with him."

"But you know Jenks?"

"We've played poker a time or two at the same table," Ryker said. "He's not a dangerous man, but he's good at what he does."

"What about you?"

"What about me?"

"Are you good at what you do?"

"There's one way to find out."

Clint shook his head.

"I don't want to find out at the cost of a life, Ryker," Clint said. "I want you to tell me."

"All right, then," the younger man said. "Yes, I am good at what I do."

"Then the job's yours if you want it."

"I'll have to meet the three women, and I'll need to be able to work with them. They'll have to do what I tell them to do, when I tell them. Is that going to be a problem?"

Thinking about Jolie, Clint lied and said, "Hey, no problem at all."

TWENTY-TWO

Clint told Ryker to give him ten minutes before coming upstairs to the second floor.

"What room?"

"I'm not sure what room we'll be in, but I'll leave the door open. You'll find it."

"All right."

"Have a beer while you're waiting," Clint said, standing up. "On me."

"I think I will."

Clint extended his hand, and Ryker stood up and took it.

"This should be interesting," Clint said.

"I'm counting on it," Ryker said.

Clint went upstairs. The two rooms they'd been given were twenty-one and twenty-two. He knocked on twenty-one first, and the door was opened by Jolie. Behind her, on the bed, he saw Marie.

"Where's Gaby?" he asked.

"She is in room twenty-two," Jolie said.

"I'll get her and be right back. We have to talk."

He went to the other room and knocked. When Gaby answered, he said, "Come next door. I have to talk to the three of you."

"But—"

He took her hand and pulled her down the hall to room twenty-one. Once they were all in the same room he explained that a man named Ryker would be coming up in a few minutes to meet them.

"He is going to look after you while I'm out looking for Henri's killer."

"Can we trust him?" Gaby asked.

"There is no reason not to."

"Do you know him?" Jolie asked.

"He was very highly recommended by someone I trust," Clint said.

"I would prefer that it was someone I trust," Jolie said.

"We trust you, Clint," Gaby said. "If you trust this man Ryker, we will, too." She punctuated her remark with a hard look at Jolie.

"He should be here any minute," Clint said. "If he's going to do this, he's going to need your cooperation. It's not easy protecting one person, let alone three. You're going to have to do as he says. Is that clear?"

He was looking directly at Jolie.

"We understand," she said coldly.

"Listen to him as you would to me," Clint said.

"All right," Gaby said.

"Marie?" Clint said.

She looked startled.

"Do you understand?"

"Oh, yes."

"And you agree?"

She looked at Gaby, who nodded.

"Yes, I do."

"Good."

Clint heard someone in the hall. He stepped outside and saw Ryker coming toward him.

"Right here," he said, and stepped back into the room.

When Ryker came in Clint was watching the women. As Ryker entered it was plain on their faces that they all liked the way he looked. Actually, it was Jolie who seemed particularly impressed, which surprised Clint, but made him glad. She was the one he expected trouble from. Maybe now it wouldn't come.

"Ladies, this is Ryker," he said. He introduced them from left to right. "Gabrielle, Marie, and Jolie."

"Ladies," Ryker said, "it's my pleasure."

None of them said anything. They put their hands behind their backs and acted shy.

"I'm going to let the four of you get acquainted," Clint said. "Ryker, I'll wait down in the saloon."

"Right."

Clint looked at all three girls and said, "Remember what I said."

The four of them remained silent until Clint left the room.

TWENTY-THREE

Ryker studied the three women for a moment. They were all stunning, and the little blonde sitting on the bed was already sending him hot messages with her eyes, but the one that interested him was the black girl, Jolie. While not as blatantly sexy as Marie, and not as truly beautiful as Gabrielle, she was to him the most interesting-looking.

"I don't know what he told you," Ryker said, "but as I understand it, I am here to keep the three of you alive."

"How do you intend to do that?" Jolie asked.

He looked directly at her.

"The best way I can."

"Would you risk your life for us?"

"Of course."

"You must be getting paid a great deal of money," she said.

"Jolie!" Gaby scolded her.

"It's all right," Ryker assured her. "As a matter of fact, I don't know what I'm getting paid for this."

"Why not?" Jolie asked.

"I told Mr. Adams I would do it as a favor."

"Why would you do that?" Jolie asked.

"Because he's the friend of a friend."

"But you are getting paid?"

"He insists on paying me."

"But you don't know how much?" Marie asked.

"No, I don't," Ryker said. "I'm leaving that up to him."

"You trust him that much?" Jolie asked.

"Like I said, he's the friend of a friend."

"Would you die for us?" Marie asked.

He looked at her and smiled. His smile made butterflies in her stomach. She thought he was even more handsome than her sweet boy on the ship.

"I hope it won't come to that," he said.

"But if it did?"

He looked directly at Marie this time and said, "For you I would die."

The butterflies in her stomach took flight while Gaby and Jolie exchanged an amused smile.

Clint was standing at the bar this time when Ryker walked in.

"Beer?" Clint asked.

"Please."

"How did it go?"

"It went fine," Ryker said. "We came to an understanding."

"You're going to have your work cut out for you," Clint said.

"I know."

"That Jolie, she's not the most cooperative person in

the world. She's got something against men.''

"Really?" Ryker asked. "I didn't notice. I think we're going to get along fine.''

"Good.''

"I have some questions for you, though.''

"Let's have them.''

"How do we work this? Where do I stay?''

"In the hotel," Clint said. "You can bunk in with me.''

"What room are you in?''

"Down the hall from them," Clint said. "Room twenty-eight.''

"Is there something going on between you and one of the girls?''

"Why do you ask?''

"I just thought I sensed something between you and Gabrielle," Ryker said. "I like to get the relationships cleared up right at the beginning . . . so I don't make any mistakes.''

Clint hesitated before answering.

"Something did start with Gaby and me, before the murder. I don't know how it will progress from here on out, though.''

"Could it get serious?''

"I don't think so," Clint said. "When this is over they'll be heading back to France, and I'll be leaving San Francisco. I don't think there's room for anything to get serious.''

"All right," Ryker said. His beer came and he made quick work of it. "I'll go and get some gear and be back in an hour.''

"Good," Clint said. "I'll be ready to go out just about

then. Uh, about you sleeping, I can spell you—''

"If you don't mind," Ryker said, "I have someone who can do that for me."

"Oh? Listen, like I said, I'm footing the bill—''

"He won't cost you anything," Ryker said. "He'll do it as a favor to me."

Clint thought that favors were flying around pretty thick in the air. He wondered what Farrell had told Ryker about him.

"Thanks for the beer," Ryker said. "I'll see you in a little while."

Clint raised his half empty mug and watched as Ryker went out the door to the street. He seemed like an intelligent, competent young man. He only hoped that Ryker was a good judge of his own worth, since he had only the man's word that he was good at what he did.

TWENTY-FOUR

Ryker returned as promised and freed Clint to leave the hotel. Before leaving, though, Clint decided to pick the younger man's brain a little more.

"What do you know about a man named Bell?" he asked.

"Harvey Bell?"

Clint nodded, even though he wasn't sure if Goodman had said Bell's first name was Harvey.

"Just what I've heard. He runs with an older fella called John. He's about your age, I think. From what I hear Bell's rotten, but John, he's bad."

"That's all you know?"

"That's it. I don't know either one of them personally."

Clint was disappointed.

"Okay, thanks."

"Maybe Duke knows something more about them."

"I'll have to ask him. You can go to work, Ryker."

"Sure."

"And thanks for helping out."

"Like I said, it'll be interesting working with you, Mr. Adams."

"Just call me Clint, okay?" Clint said.

"Sure . . . Clint."

As Ryker started away, Clint said, "Wait a minute."

"Yeah?"

"I don't know when I'll be back," Clint said. "Maybe I should know something about this other fellow you're going to use to spell you."

"Oh, sure," Ryker said. "His name's Quincy, he's about my age."

"What's he look like?"

"He's black," Ryker said. "You can't miss him."

Clint was about to object, saying that a black man would be too noticeable, then realized that being noticeable was not a bad thing for a bodyguard.

"Okay, thanks. I'll watch for him."

"I probably won't need him today. By late tomorrow I should be getting tired, though."

"You won't get sleepy till then?"

"I don't sleep much, Clint."

"Okay. I'll probably see you later, then."

Ryker went upstairs and Clint went outside. He stood in front of the hotel and took a deep breath. He still hadn't gotten any gambling done since he got to town, and it didn't look good for the immediate future. He tried to spot Sammy Jenks but couldn't. He decided to let the man follow him back to the Red Haven, where he'd find out from Garland just what the hell was going on.

•   •   •

When Clint Adams walked into the Red Haven, Sammy Jenks was confused about what to do. Should he follow him in or wait outside? After all, this was Jenks's home base. He certainly wouldn't look out of place inside. He finally decided to sit in a wooden chair just outside the door. He could still see Adams from there and wouldn't look out of place.

TWENTY-FIVE

Clint entered the Red Haven and went right to the bar, where the same bartender was wiping the bar top, probably with the same rag.

"Help ya?" the man asked.

"I want to see Garland."

The bartender looked up and down the bar.

"If you're looking for Sammy, he's outside. He followed me here."

"Huh," the bartender said.

"Tell Garland I'm here."

Again the bartender looked up and down the bar, as if he was looking for someone to send on the errand.

"Oh, for Chrissake," Clint said. He walked to the batwing doors, reached outside, and grabbed Sammy Jenks by the shirtfront. He yanked the man out of his seat and into the saloon.

"I want to see Garland," Clint said to both of them. "Somebody go and tell him."

The two men exchanged a glance, and then the bartender jerked his head and Sammy Jenks went to deliver the message.

"How'd you spot Sammy?" the bartender asked while they waited. "He's really good at following people."

"I guess he needs a little more practice," Clint said. He didn't bother telling the man how he knew that Jenks was following him. Let them all think that the man was slipping some.

Jenks reappeared and said glumly to Clint, "You can go down. You remember the way?"

"I remember."

As Clint started past him, Jenks touched his arm.

"How'd you spot me?"

"Maybe you're getting sloppy."

"No," Jenks said, with a shake of his head, "no I ain't."

Clint left him there, wondering.

He went down the steps and knocked on the door. It was opened and he was admitted. He found Garland in his office.

"Ah, Clint, good. Have you come to gamble, or have you thought of something I can do for you?"

"You can get your man off my trail, Garland—or better yet, tell me why he's there."

"Now, calm down. I hear you've had some trouble. Maybe I can help."

"I want to know why you are having me followed."

"I'm not having you followed, Clint," the man said, "I'm having you watched."

"What's the difference?"

"I feel obligated to Rick to keep an eye on you, make sure you're safe."

"I've been keeping myself safe for years, Garland. I don't need any help doing it."

"Call me Eddie, Clint."

"If I see your man again, Eddie, I'm going to send him back to you with a broken leg."

Garland looked offended.

"I was just trying to be helpful, Clint."

"You want to be helpful?"

"Very much."

"Okay," Clint said, "tell me what you know about two men named Bell and John."

Garland smiled.

"That's easy. Bell's a scum. Preys on anyone weaker than him."

"Does he live in San Francisco?"

"Sort of. He's here about half the time. Other times he's—well, wherever he is, he's still looking for weak people to steal from."

"And John?"

"John is a puzzle."

"Why?"

"Well, I shouldn't say he's a puzzle, but that it's puzzling why he's even with Bell. He's a bad man, that's for sure, but he's not the scum that Bell is. He's tougher than Bell, and smarter."

"So what's your theory?" Clint asked. "Why is he with Bell?"

"John has been around awhile."

"He looks like he's in his forties."

"He's in his mid-forties, but don't let that fool you. He hasn't slowed down any."

"Good with a gun?"

"Not in your class, but good, yes. His weapon of choice, though, is a knife."

"A knife? How good is he with a knife?"

"Like a surgeon."

"And the other two men with them?"

Garland waved a hand and said, "Dirt. Every so often they pick up a new man or two, but they never last. The partnership is Bell and John."

"Okay, where can I find them?"

"If they're in town," Garland said, "try the Market Street area. That's the best I can do."

"Not the Barbary Coast? That's where I ran into them last."

"They'll work the Coast, but they don't stay there. Market Street."

"Okay," Clint said, "you've been helpful."

"I can be more helpful. Just let me know."

"Just keep Sammy off my tail," Clint said.

"Before you go," Garland said, "I'm interested. How did you spot him? Sammy is usually very good."

"Maybe he's just getting sloppy in his old age."

Garland frowned.

"The boy is only twenty-four."

Clint shrugged and said, "Some people age faster than others." Then he left.

TWENTY-SIX

Clint went back to talk to Duke Farrell about Bell and John and the others. He didn't know why he hadn't asked Farrell about them before. The man seemed to have his finger on the very pulse of San Francisco most of the time, a talent which was probably the main reason why Tracker wanted him for a partner.

There was a man behind the front desk instead of the redhead this time. Clint told him his name and that he wanted to talk to Farrell, and then went to wait in the dining room over a cup of coffee. While waiting he realized how hungry he was and decided to order dinner.

The waiter was putting his food in front of him when Duke Farrell entered the dining room.

"There won't be any charge for Mr. Adams's dinner, Lloyd," he said to the man.

"Very good, Mr. Farrell."

"Thank you," Clint said.

Farrell sat opposite him.

"Did you meet Ryker?"

"I did. He's already on the job."

"Good," Farrell said, "I hope it all works out."

"I do, too."

"I suspect you didn't come back here just for a free meal," the smaller man said. "What else can I do for you?"

"I'm looking for two men."

"Who?"

"One is named Harvey Bell," Clint said, "the other one I only know as John."

"I know who they are."

"Good. What I want to know is where they are. Garland already told me he thought they might be in the Market Street area."

"That's a possibility," Farrell said. "I can check on that for you."

"I thought I'd go down there and have a look around," Clint said. "Maybe just walk around some and see what I could see."

"Without somebody to back you up?"

"The way I figure it, if they see me alone they might be easier to find."

"Suit yourself," Farrell said. "I can check around the rest of the city, just in case you don't run across them."

"I'd appreciate it," Clint said.

"You figure they're the killers?"

Clint shrugged as he cut into his steak. For a moment he felt guilty about eating while the women were back at the hotel, probably starving.

"I figure they're worth talking to," Clint said, "and so do the police."

"Who's working on the killing?"

"Lieutenant Goodman. Know him?"

"Actually, I do," Farrell said. "He's a good enough cop. You wouldn't want to get in his way, though."

"I'll try not to."

"Why not just leave it to him, Clint?" Farrell asked.

"Leaving my fate in the hands of others is not something I can do, Duke."

Farrell nodded his understanding.

"That's one of the ways you and Tracker are a lot alike."

"There are others?"

Farrell smiled.

"A few."

He stood up.

"I'll leave you to finish your meal. I'll see what I can turn up and send a message to your hotel."

"I appreciate it, Duke."

"Don't mention it."

As Farrell started to walk away, Clint said, "You'll have to tell me about them sometime."

"About what?"

"Those few things we have in common. Tracker and me."

"Oh," Farrell said, "those. We'll see."

TWENTY-SEVEN

Clint left the hotel and considered taking a cab to the Market Street area. He decided against it, though, because it was starting to get dark. He'd be better off starting out fresh in the morning. Instead, he told the cab to take him to the Maxwell Hotel.

When he got to the Maxwell it was dark. He went directly to the second floor and saw Ryker sitting on a chair in the hall.

"Evenin'," Ryker said.

"Hello," Clint said. He stopped right by the man, in front of Marie and Jolie's room. "How are they?"

"They're fine."

"All in here?"

Ryker shook his head.

"Just Marie and Jolie are inside."

"They must be hungry."

"They're not."

"You took them down to the dining room?"

"No," Ryker said, "I had the hotel bring food up here to them."

"That was a good idea." Clint was impressed.

"Don't be impressed with me," Ryker said. "It was Gaby's idea. She had me go down and get the manager and bring him up here, and then she charmed him into sending the food up. She's quite a gal."

"Yes, she is. How are you holding up?"

"The job's just started," Ryker said. "I'm fine."

Clint didn't see a rifle, but Ryker was wearing a handgun.

"I can use it," Ryker said, as if reading Clint's mind.

"I'll take your word for it."

"How did you do today?"

"With what?"

"I assume you're looking for the men who killed your friend, the Frenchman."

"You've been talking to the girls."

"Isn't that allowed?"

"Oh, sure it is," Clint said. "I didn't mean anything by the remark. I may have a lead on them. I'm going down to the Market Street area tomorrow for a look around."

"You could probably use somebody to watch your back," Ryker said. "I could have Quincy stay here so I can go with you."

"I'm going to try to draw them out, Ryker," Clint said. "If you see me alone that will be easier to do."

"There're four of them, aren't there?" Ryker asked.

"Yes," Clint said, "but two of them don't figure to be a problem."

"And the other two?"

"I'm pretty sure I can take my chances."

"Pretty sure?"

"Well . . . sure."

"It must be nice to be that confident."

"I know what I can do," Clint said.

"Well, let me know if you change your mind."

"I will. Thanks for the offer."

Clint started down the hall toward his own room, then stopped and turned.

"Did you say Gaby was in her room?"

"No," Ryker said, "I didn't. I just said she wasn't in this room."

Clint stared at the younger man for a few moments until he finally caught on.

"I'll see you later, then."

"Are you in for the night?" Ryker asked.

"I'm not sure," Clint said, and continued down the hall to his own room.

The door was locked so he used his key. When he entered, Gaby sat up in his bed. The lamp on the wall was turned up slightly, so that a soft, yellow light bathed her, turning her skin golden.

"How'd you get in here?" he asked.

"The manager let me in," she said.

"You managed to get food from him, and this?"

"It was not hard," she said. "He is very eager to please."

"I see."

She tossed the sheet away from her then, baring much more than just her shoulders, and said, "I am eager to please, too."

TWENTY-EIGHT

Clint was eager to let Gaby please, so he took off his clothes and got into bed with her. She was all over him immediately, her mouth and hands anxious for him. She slithered down between his legs and took him in her mouth even before he was fully hard. He swelled in her mouth and she moaned appreciatively as he grew. She cradled his testicles with one hand and encircled the base of his penis with the other. She began moving her head up and down, riding him that way, wetting him thoroughly. When he was ready to come, she knew it and used her hand to stop him. She did this several times and the pleasure was exquisite. Time and again he felt himself swell to where he thought he would burst, only to be stopped by her.

"That's enough, that's enough," he said to her after a while.

She looked up at him from between his legs, a sly smile on her face. She touched him with her hand, rubbing him, and suddenly he exploded, just like that. The sensation made him catch his breath, and his semen shot up onto his belly.

"My . . . God!" he shouted.

She laughed and went to work cleaning him avidly with her tongue. Afterward she lay in the crook of his arm, playing with his flaccid penis, waiting for it to rise again.

"You're going to have a long wait," he told her.

"I don't think so," she said into his ear.

And she was right. Five minutes later he was between her legs, driving into her like some raging bull while she urged him on in French. When he was about to explode again, he pulled out and, despite her protests, slid down between her legs to give her some of what she had given him earlier. When she was finally begging him in French—her tone giving away her meaning—he mounted her again, rammed himself into her, and continued to ride her like that, almost mindlessly, until once again he cried out. . . .

"We are suited to one another, you and I," she said later. Again she was lying in his arms, but this time her hand was resting on his belly.

"You think so?"

She laughed.

"I know so. Most men would have been finished after what I did to you, but you gave me some of my—what do you call it?—my own medicine."

"That kind of medicine could cause somebody a heart attack, Gaby."

"Oh, but what a way to die, no?"

"What a way to die, yes," he said.

"Tell me about your day."

"There isn't much to tell. I'm going to go out looking for those men tomorrow."

"The men from the dock? The animals?"

"Yes. I might have a lead on where they are."

"And you will take this other man, Ryker, with you, yes?"

"No," Clint said. "He will stay here with you and Marie and Jolie. That's his job."

"Then you will go after these men alone?"

"I will be careful, I promise," he said. "If I don't go alone they might not let themselves be found."

"Ah, but if they see you alone they will think, we are four and he is one, yes?"

"Yes."

She slapped him hard on the stomach, a stinging blow that made him yell, "Hey!"

"And they will be right. They are four and you are one. You are being foolish."

"I am not being foolish," he said, rubbing the reddening skin of his stomach. "I am baiting a trap."

"And it will close on you."

"Gabrielle," he said, his tone scolding, "I do not try to tell you how to model, do I?"

"No," she said, "but that is what I do."

"Well, this is what I do," he said.

"Ah, the famous legend, eh?"

"That's right."

She lay back in his arms.

"If you get killed, I will never forgive you."

"I'll keep that in mind."

They lay like that for a few moments before Clint spoke again.

"Maybe you better go back to your room, Gaby."

"Why?"

"Well, it's early, and I'm not ready to go to sleep yet. I want to go downstairs for a while."

"I will wait for you here."

"But—"

"Jolie might want to use my room."

"What for?"

"For her and that Ryker man, silly."

"Jolie and Ryker?" he asked, surprised. "Already?"

"Did it take you so long to take me to your bed?" she asked.

"But . . . Jolie hates men."

"She does not hate them," Gaby said. "She mistrusts them."

"What makes you think—"

"I see the way he looks at her and the way she looks at him."

"I thought Marie was making eyes at him."

"She was," Gaby said, "but he was looking at Jolie, not Marie."

"How will that make Marie feel?"

"Marie cannot have every good-looking man that she sees," Gaby said. "She must learn this."

"Well, she won't be learning it tonight," Clint said, sitting up and reaching for his clothes.

"And why not?" Gaby asked.

"Because Ryker's job is to watch the three of you, not sleep with one of you."

"Oh, so only you can sleep with one of us?"

"Yes—I mean, no—that's not what I mean."

"Perhaps the young Mr. Ryker would like to sleep with more than one of us."

He looked at her and said, "Is that a threat?"

She looked away, teasing him, and said, "I could make him look at me the way he looks at Jolie."

"On second thought," he said, putting his hand on her thigh, "why don't you just wait right here for me?"

She laughed, clapped her hands together, and said, "An excellent idea. I'm glad you thought of it."

TWENTY-NINE

When Clint stepped out of his room, Ryker was right where he'd left him, sitting on a chair in front of the room where Marie and Jolie were.

"Guess you weren't in for the night, huh?" Ryker asked.

"I guess not. Do you want anything when I come back? A beer? Maybe some coffee?"

"A pot of coffee would be good. Thanks."

"Sure."

But Clint didn't move right away.

"Something on your mind?" Ryker asked.

"Gaby mentioned that she saw something pass between you and Jolie?"

Ryker frowned.

"We didn't pass anything—"

"She meant a look," Clint said, cutting him off, "or a glance."

"Oh, I see what you mean."

"Now, I saw Marie giving you the eye."

"Oh, I saw that, too," Ryker said, "but I'm not interested in Marie—I mean, if she walked out here naked I might be, but other than that . . .''

"And what about Jolie?"

"Now her I find interesting."

"And according to Gaby she finds you interesting."

"That's good to hear."

"Is that going to cause a problem, Ryker?"

"Not for me," the younger man said. "How about you? Is it a problem for you?"

"Not if it doesn't interfere with the safety of the girls."

"We're thinking the same way, then."

"Well, that's good."

"Yes, it is."

Clint still didn't leave.

"Is there something else?"

"There's something I should probably tell you about Jolie."

"What's that?"

"She's been mistreated by men all her life," Clint explained. "She's very mistrusting of men—hates them, actually . . . or so I thought."

"Thanks for the warning."

"I just thought it might be something you should keep in mind when, uh, dealing with her."

"I will," Ryker said. "Is there anything else?"

"No . . . uh, I guess not . . . except . . . how do you take your coffee?"

Clint went down to the casino portion of the hotel. As befitted its location just off Portsmouth Square the casino fell just short of the ambience that the top hotels in the

Square offered. There was plenty of crystal and mahogany and leather, but certainly not enough to compare with the Alhambra or the Dodge House.

There was a very long bar off to one side of the room. Clint walked to it and found a place very easily. With the number of gaming tables in the room, there was plenty of space to stand at the bar.

He ordered a beer and drank it with his back leaning against the bar, taking a good look at the room. There was a section of tables where poker games were going on, but they all had house dealers. He tried to stay away from house dealers unless he was playing in some sort of tournament. He preferred private games where the deal moved around the table a player at a time. If a player was going to cheat, he could do so only once, on his own deal. A house dealer could cheat every time he dealt.

All around him he heard the murmur of voices, punctuated by a shout and a cheer whenever someone hit their number on a roulette wheel or was dealt blackjack. He wished that he was there just to gamble, so he could immerse himself in what was going on. He knew, though, that even if he sat down to play poker he'd be thinking about the murder of Henri LeConte, the danger to the women, and the fact that he, as well as they, were suspects in the murder.

He was still too wide awake to go to sleep, though, even after an energetic session with Gaby. He was one of those men who was made more awake by sex, rather than lulled to sleep by it. He decided that he would while away some time playing blackjack. He didn't particularly like the game, but it *was* a game where he'd be able to handle the cards. He finished his beer and moved away from the bar in search of a likely table.

He had been playing blackjack for an hour and was only forty dollars ahead. Since he was not a blackjack player per se, he did not adhere to all of the so-called "rules" of blackjack which governed the game. He hit when he felt like it and stayed when he felt like it, preferring to follow his instincts.

For instance, he was dealt twelve against a dealer's four showing and he hit rather than stood. Under normal circumstances a player would stand, figuring that the dealer, with fourteen being his best hand, would have to hit and likely would bust. Except that in this instance he drew a nine, which gave him twenty-one, and the dealer drew a three, giving him seventeen.

"How did you know?" the man sitting next to him asked. He had stayed with fifteen, thus losing the hand when the dealer did not bust.

A man at the far end of the table, however, cursed loudly and complained that had Clint not drawn a card the dealer would have gotten his nine, causing him to bust, since Clint was the last player to draw before the dealer did.

The argument had merit, except that to Clint's mind he was playing *his* hand, not the hands of the rest of the players. In that instance he felt that taking a card would be good for him, regardless of how good or bad it would be for the rest of the players.

Now, an hour later and even, he felt it was time to push.

He watched the cards as the dealer dealt the next hand.

The first player drew card against an eight and a seven and busted with another seven. The second player, a handsome woman in her thirties, stood with sixteen, which she fashioned from a six, a seven, and a fortunate draw of a three.

The man to Clint's immediate right looked at Clint, obviously wishing he had the other's instincts, for he was losing heavily. He was sitting with a ten—or jack—and a four and was obviously undecided what to do.

Finally he said, "Hit me," and the dealer gave him an eight, busting his hand.

Clint had a nine and a deuce, giving him eleven. His bet was the table minimum of twenty dollars.

"Double," he said, and put up another twenty. He had been waiting for the opportunity to double his bet. The dealer nodded and promptly dealt him a king, giving him a winning count of twenty-one. The only way he would not win was if the dealer also turned over twenty-one—which he did not do. He drew to a sixteen, caught a three, which gave him nineteen. He beat the woman, but paid Clint forty dollars, which gave Clint eighty for the hand.

The dealer collected the cards and called for bets to be made. Clint left the eighty dollars on the table, while the other players bet twenty.

"You're gonna let that ride, right?" the man to Clint's right asked.

"That's right."

"You must have a good feeing."

"I do," Clint said. Then he added, "Blackjack."

The man whistled soundlessly, impressed with the bet. He was obviously a merchant or a clerk who was playing

with scared money and was therefore losing. Clint knew
for a fact that if you were afraid to lose, you rarely ever
won.

"Cards comin' out," the dealer said.

"Come on, come on, deal," the first man said.

Clint looked down the table and caught the eye of the
woman. She had been looking at his bet and now looked
at him and smiled. He returned the smile. If Gaby had not
been waiting in his bed, he might have shown more interest.

The first three players all drew cards and busted. The
dealer gave Clint a king of spades, and then an ace of
hearts.

"Blackjack."

THIRTY

"I don't believe it," the man sitting to Clint's right said. "He called it. He called blackjack." He turned and repeated it to the other players. "He called blackjack."

The dealer gave Clint his chips, counting out one hundred and twenty dollars, which gave Clint two hundred in front of him, all profit. He could have quit right there and then, but he had decided to push. The way he played, he considered three hands in a row a good run, and he had just won two.

The others put up their bets. The first man, growing even more surly in the face of Clint's good fortune, bet fifty. The woman and the other man bet twenty.

Clint left the two hundred where it was.

"Jesus," the man next to him said. "Again?"

Clint smiled.

"Third time's the charm."

"Blackjack again?"

"You never know if you don't try."

"Jesus," the man said, "he's bettin' two hundred dollars."

Somebody heard that and passed it on and before long there was a small crowd of people watching the game.

The man on Clint's right nodded to himself, looked down at his bet, and then quickly and carefully added another ten-dollar chip. He smiled nervously at Clint and folded his arms in front of him on the table.

The first man was dealt twelve and drew to it. He got a ten to go with it, busting at twenty-two.

"God*damn it*," he swore.

The woman was dealt seventeen and stayed.

The other man, who had nervously increased his bet to thirty dollars, was dealt an ace of diamonds and then a king of clubs. Blackjack.

"I won!" he exclaimed. "Look, I got blackjack."

When the dealer gave him his money he would have seventy-five dollars. He was thrilled.

"Congratulations," the woman said.

"Goddamn!" the first man muttered.

All eyes turned to Clint's two-hundred-dollar bet.

The dealer gave him a ten of hearts, and then dropped an ace of spades right on top of it.

"He did it again," the man next to Clint said. "Oh my God, we both got blackjack."

The dealer gave Clint his chips, giving him a profit on the night of five hundred dollars.

"Thank you," he said to the dealer.

The woman caught Clint's eye and said, "Nice bet."

"Thanks."

"Nice bet, my ass," the man in the first seat said loudly, "somethin' ain't right here."

There was a heavy silence at the table suddenly as players and spectators looked at the man.

Clint noticed for the first time that he was a burly man with very dark black hair and a heavy shadow of stubble on his face. His eyes were tiny with dark eyebrows over them, and he was now staring at the dealer.

"Sir?" the dealer asked. "Is there a problem?"

The dealer was himself not a small man, blond and tall, though not as heavy through the shoulders as the burly man. He was about thirty-five, while the complainer was in his forties.

"You're damn right there's a problem," the man said loudly. He was not drunk, just loud and upset. "I been sitting here for three damned hours and I ain't got blackjack once. You just dealt it twice this hand, and you gave it to that fella on the end two hands in a row."

"Sometimes it happens like that, sir," the dealer said, as pleasantly as he could.

"No, it don't sometimes happen," the man said, "not just when he's lettin' his money ride." He was pointing to Clint when he said this.

"I don't understand this," Clint said, causing the man to look at him. "Who are you accusing of cheating, friend, the dealer or me?"

The man sneered and said, "It's probably both of you. I been watchin' you, *friend*, and you ain't been behind once since you sat down."

"Maybe that's because I'm a good player and you're not," Clint suggested.

"That's a lie," the man said. "You ain't even a blackjack player. You don't play by the rules."

"I play by my rules," Clint said.

"Two blackjacks in a row," the man said, "with that much money bet just ain't normal. Hell, you're the house! You ain't supposed to lose to a bet like that."

"Sometimes we do, sir," the dealer said.

"Okay, then," the man said, "I tell you what. I'm gonna bet a hundred dollars this time." He put up a hundred dollars worth of chips. "I want you to deal me a blackjack like you dealt him."

"I don't deal blackjack on purpose, sir."

"Just do it," the man said, " 'cause if you don't I'm gonna mess up that pretty face of yours."

"There's no need to get nasty—" the woman started, but the man cut her off.

"You shut up. This ain't none of your business."

"Hey," the man next to Clint said, "you shouldn't be talkin' to a lady like that."

"You shut up, too," the man said. He looked at the dealer and said, "Deal."

"Is there a problem here?" a man asked, stepping out from what now had become a crowd.

"Who are you?"

"I manage this casino," the man said. He was average height, slightly portly, with a heavy mustache and receding chin. He was not the same man who managed the hotel, but that was often the case with hotel/casinos.

"My name is Willoughby. And you are?"

"Gettin' impatient," the man said.

The dealer briefly explained the problem to the manager, who nodded his understanding.

"Very well, Jim, deal the cards."

"Bets up," Jim, the dealer, said to the others.

"No," the man said, "just to me."

Jim looked at Willoughby.

"Go ahead."

Jim dealt the man a ten and a nine.

"That ain't blackjack," the man complained,

"Nevertheless, it's not a bad hand," the manager said. "Don't you want to play it?"

The man thought a moment, then said, "Okay. I'll play it."

The dealer showed a five, and when he turned over his hole card it was an ace. He had sixteen or six since an ace counted as one or eleven. Either way he had to draw a card, and when he did it was a four, giving him twenty or ten. Naturally, he called it twenty.

"You lose," the manager said to the man, "and I think it's time for you to leave."

THIRTY-ONE

"You're all cheats," the man said. He pushed off his stool and Clint knew he was going to go for his gun. While the man pushed the manager away from him violently, Clint came off his stool as quickly as he could. The irate man took a step back and started to go for his gun. The casino bouncers were too far away to do anything, and the place was too crowded for them to shoot. The only one close enough to intercede was Clint.

The man was clearing leather when Clint reached him. He put his hand on top of the other man's hand and shoved his gun back into his holster.

"You don't want to do that."

"Get off me!" The man's breath was foul.

"You'll be dead before you can pull the trigger. Look around you."

The man did. By now the bouncers—three of them—had reached the table and they all had their weapons out and pointed at the man.

"I'm going to remove your gun," Clint said. "If you let me do it, you'll get out of here alive."

128

The man looked at Clint and then back at the bouncers. When Clint lifted his hand, the man dropped his away from the gun. Clint removed his weapon and handed it to the nearest bouncer.

"Take him outside," Willoughby said to the bouncers.

"Should we call for the police, Mr. Willoughby?" one of them asked.

"You don't need the police," Clint said, before anyone else could speak. "He won't come back . . . will you?"

"No," the man said grudgingly, "I ain't comin' back."

"See?" Clint said.

"No police," Willoughby said to the bouncers, "just take him outside."

"Yessir."

"Unload his gun before you give it back," Clint suggested.

"You heard the man," Willoughby said, and the bouncers nodded.

As they took the man away, the manager turned to Clint.

"Would you allow me to buy you a drink, sir?"

"Sure," Clint said, "I'm finished here."

"I will have you cashed out and the money brought to you," Willoughby said.

"Thanks."

"No, it's I who should thank you, sir. You saved us from a dangerous situation. If he had drawn his gun, some innocent people might have gotten hurt. Will you come to the bar with me?"

Clint nodded and followed the man to the bar. A path opened in the crowd for them.

"Please," Willoughby said, "go back to your gaming. The excitement is over."

At the bar Clint ordered a beer and Willoughby a brandy.

"My name is August Willoughby, by the way," the manager said.

"Clint Adams."

"Adams," the manager said. "I know the name well, sir. It's an honor to have you in my establishment. Are you staying at the hotel?"

"I am."

"Then allow me to see to your bill," Willoughby said.

"That's not necessary—"

"Nonsense," the man said. "You've done us a great service. The least we can do is make you our guest. The remainder of your stay will not cost you one penny."

"Thank you, that's kind of you."

The drinks came and Willoughby handed Clint his beer.

"To you, sir, and your pleasant stay at the Maxwell Hotel."

"Thank you."

Clint had the drink with Willoughby and then a man appeared with his money.

"You did well, Mr. Adams," Willoughby said.

"I was lucky," Clint said, pocketing his money. "I don't usually play blackjack. Poker is my game."

"Ah," Willoughby said, his eyes shining, "then perhaps I can interest you in a private game while you're here?"

"I have some business to finish up," Clint said, "but

after that I'd be very interested."

"Good, good," the man said, "just come and see me when you're ready. I must go back to work now." He put out his hand. "Again, you have our thanks."

"Glad I was able to help."

The manager walked away and Clint left the casino and entered the hotel lobby. He'd made some money, had some excitement, and now that he was a guest of the hotel—in the truest sense of the word—it made it much easier for him to pay for the two rooms the women were using. In fact, if he moved Gaby into his room permanently, he'd only have to pay for the one room, which made a lot of sense to him now.

"Excuse me?"

He turned and saw the woman who had been at the blackjack table. Standing up she was even lovelier, with a blue gown showing off a deep cleavage.

"Hello."

"My name is Isabelle."

"Clint Adams."

"I know," she said. "I heard you introduce yourself to the manager. I was very . . . impressed by you back there."

"My blackjack playing is not usually impressive," he said. "It's usually a matter of luck."

"Your luck was very good tonight."

"Yes, it was."

"However, I was talking about how you handled that man."

"Oh, that," he said. "I just didn't want to see anyone get hurt."

"You move very quickly."

"I was just—"

"Do you move that quickly all the time?"

"Well," he said, recognizing now that she was flirting with him, "sometimes—"

"I move quickly, too," she said, putting her hand on his chest, "sometimes too quickly for my own good."

"Isabelle—"

"Am I being too forward," she asked, "in saying that I would very much like to go to bed with you tonight?"

Forward women did not scare Clint, and under normal circumstances he would've taken her up on her offer in a moment.

"Isabelle," he said, shaking his head and looking once again at the shadow of her cleavage, smelling the perfumed scent that came from there, "another time, another place . . ."

"You have a girl in your room, don't you?"

"How did you know?"

She laughed.

"Why else would you turn me down? Of course, I could take another room—"

"I don't think I can do that."

She smiled.

"One girl at a time, eh?"

"I'm afraid so."

"Admirable," she said, looking him up and down with regret. "I'm impressed by you more and more. Perhaps another time? If we meet again?"

"Definitely another time, Isabelle."

"Yes," she said, smiling enigmatically, "another time."

A man came out of the casino just then, a white-haired man in his sixties, and he walked toward them.

"Ah, there you are, darling."

She turned and smiled at the man.

"Hello, dear. Let me introduce you to an interesting man. Clint Adams, this is my husband, Herman Maron."

"Mr. Adams," Maron said, "a pleasure."

"My pleasure as well, sir," Clint said. It did not surprise him that Isabelle was married. She seemed the type of woman who would be willing to try anything.

"Darling, we have to be going," he said to her, ignoring Clint, obviously not knowing or caring who he was.

She turned to Clint and said, "Remember, we will meet again," and then was whisked away by her impatient husband.

"I'll remember," Clint said.

THIRTY-TWO

Clint woke up feeling guilty the next morning. After an entire night of lovemaking with Gaby he felt guilty because, from time to time, he'd found himself thinking about Isabelle, the dark-haired woman from the blackjack game. Gabrielle was an energetic and eager lover, and all of his attention should have been focused on her. This was just further proof to him that he did not—and probably would never—belong with one woman. There were just too many beautiful ones out there.

Because of his guilt he spent extra time with her in the morning. He woke first and looked down at her. Her dark hair was fanned out on the pillow around her head. She had been sleeping most of the night on her left side—when they did sleep—with him spooned up against her, so that the wrinkles in the sheets had left marks on that side of her face.

He touched her cheek where the marks were, then trailed his fingers down over her lips and chin, slid them down her neck to her breasts, where he made circles around her nipples. She stirred, moaned, and then wriggled her butt.

"Oooh," she said, keeping her eyes closed as his finger

134

touched her right nipple. He leaned over and at the same time touched his tongue to the left one. "Ahhh," she said appreciatively.

As Clint slid the sheet off of her and gazed at her pale skin he felt sorry for Ryker, who had probably spent the night on a hard chair in the hall.

Ryker could not believe his good fortune.

During the night the door to the hotel room had opened and Jolie, wearing the flimsiest of nighties, had slipped out. Right through the fabric he could see her dark nipples and suddenly he had a raging erection.

"Jolie," he said, his throat dry, "what are you doing out here?"

"We have a problem, Ryker," she said.

She pressed her back to the door as she closed it. Ryker looked up and down the hall, afraid that someone was going to see them—or her.

"You want to go to bed with me, no?"

The question startled him, but he answered it honestly.

"I want to go to bed with you, yes."

"Then we have a problem."

"What is it?"

"Marie."

"What about her?"

"She also wants to go to bed with you."

"Well, she's very pretty, but I'm interested in you, Jolie."

"I know, *mon cher*," she said, putting a hand on his shoulder, "but Marie is my friend. I would feel badly if I slept with you, knowing that she wanted you."

"So then we have a problem?"

"*Oui*, but an easily solved one."

"How?"

"Come," she said, taking his hand, "I will show you."

He stood up and let her guide him to the door. She opened it and pulled him inside. On the bed Marie was waiting, totally naked. Her body was taut, with firm, small breasts. As Ryker entered she got up on her knees and ran her hand over her body, stopping with her breasts cupped in her hands.

When Ryker turned to look at Jolie, he saw that she had dropped her nightie on the floor. She had larger breasts than Marie, though no less firm, and wide hips. She did a slow turn so he could admire her, all the while looking at him over her shoulder. She had marvelous buttocks, big and firm and smooth.

"Both of you?" he asked, his voice hoarse.

"What better way to guard both of us?" Jolie asked.

Ryker frowned a moment, wondering how Clint would feel about this. He couldn't fault Jolie's logic, though. There was no better way to guard them both than to be in the room with them.

In the same bed.

"Ryker," Marie said, drawing the name out.

Jolie moved to the bed and joined Marie on it. Her dark skin was in stark contrast to Marie's pale flesh. Seeing them side by side like that on the bed, he wasted no time in getting out of his clothes and joining them.

He did, however, keep his gun by the bed.

THIRTY-THREE

When Clint left his room, his legs were weak. This time he had thought only of Gaby as she worked on him with her mouth, bringing him to an explosion that lifted his butt off the bed.

"What are you going to do today?" she asked while he dressed. She was propped up on one elbow.

"Like I told you last night, I'm going down to the Market Street area to see if I can find Bell and John and the others."

"Alone?"

"Yes," he said, pulling his boots on. He took his gun from the bedpost and strapped it on. "We shouldn't be having this conversation again, Gaby. I'll be careful."

She flopped onto her back, arms out from her side, staring unhappily at the ceiling.

"And what do we do if you do not come back?" she asked.

"I'll be back."

"Just tell me what to do if you don't," she yelled.

He stared down at her and said, "If I don't, you will

have to place yourself in the hands of the police. I've been told that Lieutenant Goodman is a good policeman. He is the one you should talk to."

"Fine."

"But I'll be back."

"Fine."

She didn't look at him as he walked to the door and went out into the hall. He didn't see the single tear form in her right eye and roll down her cheek.

Out in the hall Clint was concerned when he didn't see Ryker at his post. He walked quickly down the hall to the door, but then something told him to stop before knocking. He put his ear to the door and heard unmistakable sounds from inside. Somebody was having some unforgettable sex.

Clint had gotten keys from the manager for all three rooms. Quietly he inserted the key into the lock, then turned the doorknob and opened the door. He opened it just far enough for him to see what was going on. Three naked bodies were writhing together on the bed. Jolie's black skin was unmistakable, and he found himself staring at her fine ass as it bobbed up and down. Briefly he saw Ryker's face, and Marie's hair, and he closed the door before they could notice him. He intended to give Ryker some grief about leaving his post.

Not right now, however. Right now he was going to let the three of them finish what they started.

THIRTY-FOUR

Market Street was teeming with humanity. The entire area was commercial, with stores and businesses and restaurants and hotels. Spotting someone here would be a miracle, which made it an ideal area for scum like Bell and John and their friends to hide out in.

Clint walked from one end to the other and back again, keeping an eye out for a familiar face. He had the features of all four men permanently embedded in his memory. He only needed to spot one. Was that too much to ask? Of course, coincidence was something he hated, so naturally it would rear its ugly head in the person of Lieutenant Goodman.

Goodman would not be hard to spot anywhere, not even here. When Clint saw the big policeman up ahead of him, his first instinct was to try to melt into the crowd, but then he decided against it. He decided to see how the policeman reacted to coincidence.

He kept walking, knowing that the policeman would eventually turn around and spot him. The man seemed to be alone, scanning the faces in the crowd for . . . who?

Was he looking for Bell and John as well, or was he there for a different reason altogether?

Clint was almost abreast of the man when Goodman saw him.

"What the hell are you doing here, Adams?" he demanded. He was not happy.

"I'm taking in the sights, Lieutenant."

"On Market Street?"

"There seems to be a lot to see."

"Only there's too many people in the way to see it," Goodman said.

"What are you doing here, Lieutenant?"

"My job."

"Quite a coincidence running into you."

"Is it?" Goodman asked. "I'm not a man who takes kindly to coincidence, Adams."

"That's funny," Clint said, "I don't like them much, myself."

Goodman looked around, then said, "Let's duck in here," and pulled Clint into a small café. They were seated and ordered a pot of coffee.

"Is this on you, Lieutenant?" Clint asked when the waiter brought the pot and two cups.

Goodman gave Clint a humorless smile and said, "We'll split it. I want to know what you're doing around here, Adams."

"I told you—"

"Don't give me that. You're looking for Bell and his pals."

"Well," Clint said, "if I did happen to see them here—"

"What would you do?"

"Why, I'd send for you immediately, Lieutenant."

"I doubt that very much. You didn't get your reputation—"

"What reputation might that be, Lieutenant?" Clint asked, cutting the man off so quickly that Goodman was taken aback.

"Never mind. Why aren't you guarding those women if you think they're in such danger?"

Clint thought of Ryker in bed with Jolie and Marie and wondered if Gaby had discovered them. What would she do if she did? Join them?

"Believe me, Lieutenant," he said, "they're in good hands."

"Look," Goodman said, "let me level with you."

"Okay, go ahead."

"My superiors want me to close this case."

"Why?"

"Because the victim was a foreigner with no ties to the community. In other words, he was nobody."

"And if you close it, are the ladies free to leave the country?"

"That's just it," Goodman said. "I'm not closing it."

"Why not?"

"Because I want to find out who killed the poor guy, foreigner or not."

"You know, the word I got on you seems accurate."

"What word?"

"That you're a good policeman."

"Who told you that?"

"Duke Farrell."

Goodman's eyebrows went up.

"I know Farrell. He said that, huh?"

"He did. Tell me more about wanting to solve this case."

"I've got three days to close it. Also, I have no men to work with me. I'm on my own."

"That's bad."

"Yes, it is," Goodman said. "Watching your own back is always hard . . . even when you've got as wide a back as mine."

"You made a joke, Lieutenant," Clint said, surprised.

"I've been known to make a few, Adams."

"Since we're talking so civilly here, Lieutenant, why don't you just call me Clint?"

"Fine," Goodman said, "and you can call me Lieutenant . . . Clint!"

THIRTY-FIVE

"I'm asking for your help."

Clint studied the policeman for a few moments.

"Hurts to ask, doesn't it?" he asked.

"Yes, damn it, it does," Goodman said. "I shouldn't have to ask. I should be getting the help from my own department, and I'm not. That makes me madder still."

"You want to work together then?"

Clint watched the man's jaw work for a few moments before he answered. It was clear to him that the lieutenant wanted Clint to work *for* him, not with him, but the man was going to have to compromise.

"All right, damn it," he said finally. "We'll work together."

"You think that Bell and his crew are the killers?" Clint asked.

"I think they're the best suspects."

"You've discounted me and the women?"

"You."

"Not the women?"

"No."

"Why not?"

"Because a knife is a woman's weapon."

"You're saying a woman's more likely to cut someone's throat?"

"Not necessarily," Goodman said, "but it can be done. The cut was not a particularly vicious one, but it did the job. It was the kind of cut an expert might use—or a woman who didn't have much strength beyond what it took to actually kill him."

"A woman . . ." Clint said, thinking.

"A woman would have gotten close enough with no problem," Goodman said.

"So would a man with a gun," Clint pointed out, "especially if he had help."

"True."

They finished their coffee and declined the waiter's offer of another cup.

"Gentlemen, we will be needing the table for lunch," the waiter said, "if there's nothing else—"

"There is," Goodman said, showing the man his badge. "Go away."

"Yes, sir."

Goodman put his badge away.

"Do you have someone watching the hotel, Lieutenant?" Clint asked.

"I told you," Goodman said, "I have no help on this."

"Well, I thought maybe . . ."

"That I was lying so you wouldn't know your hotel was being watched?"

"Something like that."

"I'm not," the man said. "I'm on my own with this case."

"Well," Clint said, "not anymore."

THIRTY-SIX

They left the café and went back into the crowded streets.

"Instead of backing each other," Clint said, "I think we should split up."

"What good will that do?"

"We'll cover more ground."

"And when one of us finds them?"

"Follow them."

Goodman frowned.

"Look at me, Adams," he said.

"Clint."

"Clint," Goodman said. "Do I look like the type of man who could follow someone unnoticed?"

"In a crowd, maybe, and that's what we're dealing with here today."

Goodman studied Clint for a few moments.

"I get it."

"Get what?"

"You're out here as bait."

Clint didn't respond.

"You don't want to find them, you want them to find you."

Clint still remained silent.

"You figure since they saw you with the Frenchman, if they see you again they'll come after you."

"Maybe."

"I know who you are, Ad—Clint, but do you really think you can face down four men?"

"I might not have to face all four, Lieutenant."

"But you're willing to deal with that possibility?"

"Yes."

Goodman shook his head.

"It must be awful nice to have that much confidence in yourself."

Clint didn't answer.

"I've got another idea."

"I'm listening."

"They don't know me," Goodman said. "Why don't I just follow along behind you and watch?"

"You're a big man—"

"You just told me I could blend into a crowd, Clint," Goodman said. "Now which is it?"

Clint frowned, realizing he was not going to be able to get rid of the policeman.

"All right, Lieutenant," he said, "I guess that means you'll be watching my back."

Goodman smiled.

"And it couldn't be in better hands."

"I hope so."

• • •

Ryker sat up in bed and said, "Gaby."

Marie was on one side of him and Jolie on the other. He was pleasantly exhausted from their attentions. He especially liked when they were both crouched between his legs, passing his penis back and forth from mouth to mouth, sucking him earnestly, waiting to see how long he could last and who the lucky girl would be. When he exploded into Jolie's mouth, Marie was unhappy until the black girl released him. There was one spurt of semen in the air and then Marie's mouth swooped down on him.

These girls, he concluded, were *really* good friends.

But now suddenly he thought of Gaby.

"She is with Clint," Marie said, reaching for him.

"Clint was gonna go out early," Ryker said.

"Then she is in his room," Jolie said.

"Alone," Ryker said to both of them.

There was a long silence, and then Jolie said, "She will be all right, won't she?"

Ryker jumped off the bed and hurriedly started to dress.

"I don't know. That's what I have to find out."

"Come back to bed, Ryker," Marie said in a little girl voice.

Jolie also got off the bed and started to dress.

"Marie, he's right," she said. "We have to check on Gaby."

"Gaby, Gaby," Marie said with a pout, "always Gaby."

Ryker and Jolie both ignored her. As they left the room Marie was still in the bed, pouting.

•   •   •

Ryker and Jolie rushed to Clint's room and knocked on the door. There was no answer.

"Gaby?" Jolie called.

Ryker drew his gun and tried the door. It was unlocked. He turned the knob and pushed it open, then pushed Jolie away and entered.

The bed was in a state of disarray, but the room was empty. The bed could have been like that from two people having had sex on it.

"Where is she?" Jolie asked, looking into the room.

"I don't know," Ryker said. He turned and looked at Jolie. "Why would she leave the hotel, Jolie?"

The black girl shook her head in confusion and said, "I do not know."

THIRTY-SEVEN

"Clint's gonna kill me," Ryker said, shaking his head. "He trusted me."

"We just have to find her," Jolie said.

They were walking back down the hall.

"I can't believe I did this," Ryker said as they re-entered the hotel room.

"What happened?" Marie asked. She was still naked on the bed.

"Get dressed," Ryker said.

"But—"

"Get dressed!" he snapped louder.

She blinked as if slapped, got off the bed, and started to get dressed.

"Where are we going?" she asked.

"I have to find Gaby," Ryker said, "and you two have to come with me."

"Why don't we look for her separately?" Jolie asked.

"No," Ryker said, "I'm supposed to be guarding you. I can't let you go off on your own."

"But just in the hotel—"

"The answer is no, Jolie," he said. "That's final. We'll go and look for her together."

Ryker couldn't believe it. When he'd been given the chance to work with Clint Adams—the goddamned *Gunsmith*, for Chrissake!—he had jumped at it. He'd been determined to impress Clint, and now he'd lost Gaby.

"Come on, Marie," he yelled. "Get dressed."

She was dawdling.

"You don't have to yell," Marie called back.

He opened his mouth to retort, then realized that she was right. He didn't have to yell. It wasn't their fault he'd made a mess of things.

Before he could apologize he heard a voice from behind him.

"What's all the yelling?" Gaby asked. "Can't a girl get some sleep?"

Ryker turned and saw her standing in the hall with a sheet wrapped around her.

"Where did you come from?" he demanded.

"My room, where else?"

"Weren't you in Clint's room all night?"

"I was," she said, "but when he left this morning I moved to my room."

Jolie rushed to her and hugged her.

"Is that against the law?" Gaby asked, confused.

"No," Ryker said, slumping onto the bed in relief, "no, Gaby, it isn't against the law."

THIRTY-EIGHT

Clint and Goodman were about to quit when Clint saw one of the men who had been poking the three women on the dock. He didn't know his name, but he recognized him on sight. He stopped walking and waved for Goodman to join him.

"What is it?"

"Across the street," Clint said. "See him? Standing in front of the hardware store?"

"Tall man, black hat?"

"That's him. He was with Bell and John when they were bothering LeConte and the girls."

"My information says his name is either Starr or Lukas."

"Well, whichever it is, what do you want to do about it?"

"We can go one of two ways," Goodman said. "Grab him now or follow him."

"I say we follow him," Clint said. "He might lead us to the others."

"All right, but I think I should stay on this side of the

street. If he spots me behind him he's gonna know something's up.''

"I think we should both stay on this side of the street," Clint said. "We can follow him from here."

"All right," Goodman said. "Let's do it, then. He's moving."

The man started to walk and they followed along, keeping him in view from across the street. They went on like that for a few blocks and then the man crossed over to their side.

"Shit," Goodman said.

"No problem," Clint said. "Let's just cross over to the other side."

They did so and continued to follow the man in this fashion. Eventually the man stopped in front of a saloon and went in. Clint and Goodman stopped in a doorway across the street. They had come away from the Market Street area and it was less busy here. They hoped that by standing in the doorway they would not be noticed.

"Now what do we do?" Clint sad. "I can't go inside, he'll notice me."

"And in this neighborhood," Goodman said, "if I go inside there might be somebody in there I arrested once."

"We have to find out if the others are in there with him, or if he's waiting for them," Clint said.

"And maybe he's just having a drink alone," Goodman said. "Or meeting a woman."

"There's a window," Clint said. "I'll cross over and take a look. You keep your eyes open and whistle if you see anyone."

"I know what Bell and John look like," Goodman said,

"but if the third man starts coming down the block I won't know him from Adam—uh, no joke intended."

"We'll have to take that chance," Clint said. "It won't take me long to cross over and take a look. Just keep a watchful eye."

"I will," Goodman said. "Go."

Clint crossed the street and headed for the window.

Gaby got dressed and came out into the hall where Ryker was sitting. She folded her arms and leaned against the wall.

"I'm sorry if I frightened you," she said.

He looked up at her.

"It wasn't your fault," he said. "It was mine. I shouldn't have let myself get distracted. When I thought about you being alone I felt guilty. When I didn't find you in Clint's room, I built it up in my head that something was wrong. I scared myself."

"Well, you shouldn't blame yourself too much," Gaby said. "Jolie and Marie can be very distracting."

"I know," Ryker said, "but I still shouldn't have . . ."

Gaby put her hand on Ryker's shoulder to comfort him. Neither of them noticed that the door to the other room was open just a crack.

THIRTY-NINE

Clint pressed his face to the glass. For a moment he couldn't see the man. He hoped that Starr or Lukas hadn't spotted them and gone out the back way. He continued to peer inside and then he saw the man, sitting at a table by himself with a mug of beer. While Clint was watching him, he took out a pocket watch and had a look at it. Clint left the window and hurried back across the street.

"Well?" Goodman asked.

"He's sitting at a table, waiting."

"For what?"

"For his partners."

"How do you know?"

"I don't know," Clint said, "I hope."

"Well, what makes you think he's waiting?"

"He's having a beer and he's checking his watch."

"He's waiting."

"That's what I said."

"But maybe he's waiting for a woman?"

"What kind of woman would go with that man?"

"The kind you pay for."

154

"Well, there's only one way to find out, then."

"Right," Goodman said, "stay here and wait."

"Right."

"For as long as it takes."

They both backed into the doorway, which, given Goodman's size, was barely wide enough for both of them.

"It won't take long," Clint said.

"Now what makes you say that?"

"He was checking his watch."

"So?"

"So if he's checking his watch they must be due here any minute."

"Were you ever a policeman?"

"No." Clint had been a lawman years ago but never what Goodman would call a policeman. "Why?"

"Because you think like a policeman."

"Is that supposed to be a compliment?"

"The way things are going these days?" Goodman said. "I'm not so sure."

They waited about ten or fifteen minutes in silence. It was late afternoon and in this section of San Francisco the foot traffic was not at all heavy.

"We're too easy to spot," Goodman said. "And it's getting later. When there's nobody left on the street we'll be even easier to spot."

"Then we need another place to watch from."

"Yes."

"Which way would you suggest we go?"

Goodman hesitated a moment, then elevated his eyes and said, "Up."

FORTY

Using Goodman's badge as an entrée they managed to get to the roof of one of the buildings across the street from the saloon where Starr or Lukas was waiting. Now they were safe from detection. A half hour later their patience paid off.

"Look," Clint said.

"Where?"

"There, to the left, coming down the block."

"Who is it?" Goodman was squinting.

"Do you wear glasses?"

"No, why?"

"Never mind," Clint said. "It's the other man, Starr or Lukas, depending on which one is in the saloon."

As they watched, the man went right to the door of the saloon and entered. He had his arm in a sling.

"You do that to him?" Goodman asked.

Clint nodded.

"Okay," Goodman said, "now we know Starr and Lukas are inside. Let's hope they're still going to wait for Bell and John."

"They are."

"What makes you say that?"

"I can feel it."

Goodman stared at Clint.

"Are you sure you were never a policeman?"

"Never," Clint said.

They settled down to wait.

Ryker was starting to get tired. It was sooner than he had expected, but he hadn't counted on going to bed with two of the girls he was supposed to be guarding. He didn't have a watch, so he didn't know what time it was. He had told Quincy to spell him early in the evening. He wondered if it was time yet.

He couldn't help thinking about them while he was sitting alone in the hall. At one point Marie had been sitting astride him, his erection buried deep inside of her. She had her hands pressed to his stomach and was riding him up and down fiercely, moaning aloud every time she came down on him. He couldn't see her face, however, because Jolie was crouched over him, his mouth working avidly on her pussy. He had to admit to himself that he'd wondered how she would taste. He had never been with a black woman before. She was extremely sensitive, and each time his tongue touched her clitoris she had to fight back a scream. The two women were making so much noise he wondered at times if the entire hotel could hear them.

When somebody appeared at the end of the hall, it pulled him from his reverie.

"Wake you up?" his friend Quincy Jackson asked.

"Hell no," Ryker said. "What time is it, anyway?"

"Time for you to get out of here and get some rest," the big black man said.

Quincy was thirty years old and stood six foot three in his bare feet. He and Ryker had been friends for a few years and partners of sorts for the past year. Whenever one got an interesting job he usually drew the other into it, as well.

"Where are these ladies we're supposed to be protectin'?" Quincy asked.

"In these two rooms," Ryker said, jerking his thumb behind him. "I'll introduce you."

"You been sittin' out here in the hall the whole time?" Quincy asked, waggling his eyebrows.

"The whole time," Ryker lied.

"You lie," Quincy said. "You had one of 'em."

"What makes you say that?"

"I can smell it on you."

Ryker looked down at himself and sniffed.

"Plus you can't ever lie to me."

"Never mind," Ryker said, standing up. "I'm gonna introduce you. Just keep your mind on business, okay?"

"Always."

Ryker knocked first on Gaby's door. When she answered Quincy's eyebrows went up, but he said nothing.

"Gabrielle, this is Quincy. He'll be taking over while I go and get some rest."

"*Monsieur* Quincy," Gaby said, with a smile, "it is so nice of you to help us."

"Well . . ." Quincy said, and Ryker was shocked. He'd never before seen the black man at a loss for words.

"I'll be introducing him to Jolie and Marie, and then I'll be on my way."

"*Bon*," Gaby said. "You will get some well-deserved rest and be back tomorrow?"

"Yes, ma'am, I will."

"Good night, then."

She smiled at Quincy and closed the door.

"Is that the one?" Quincy asked.

"Keep your mind on business, I said."

Ryker knocked on the other door. When Jolie answered Quincy showed some real interest.

"Jolie, this is my friend Quincy."

"*Bon jour*, friend Quincy," Jolie said.

"I'd like Marie to see him, too," Ryker said. "He'll be taking over tonight."

"Marie?" Jolie called.

When Marie came to the door she was wearing a nightie that allowed both men a good look at her breasts and nipples. While she was a sight to behold, both of the men were still more interested in Jolie. Marie, meanwhile, was awed by Quincy's size.

"*Magnifique*," she said in hushed tones, devouring him with her eyes.

"Did you bring a gun?" Ryker asked.

Quincy took an old Navy Colt from behind his back and showed it to Ryker, then tucked it back into his belt.

"You ladies should be safe for the night," Ryker said to them. "You can trust Quincy. I'll see you in the morning."

"Good night, Ryker," Jolie said.

"Good night, Jolie."

Marie was still too interested in Quincy to bid Ryker good night.

"You better close the door now," Ryker said. Jolie smiled and did as she was told.

"That's the one, isn't it?" Quincy asked.

"The blonde? Marie?"

"Not the blonde. I saw the way you looked at the other one, Jolie. Man, she black an' French?" Quincy shook his head in wonder.

"Yes, she is," Ryker said, "and she's . . . special."

"You tellin' me hands off, partner?"

"Jesus," Ryker said, "how can I tell you that? I just met them myself. Goin' to bed with them was just . . ." Ryker was at a loss for words.

"Wait a minute, wait a minute," Quincy said, "let me get this straight. *Them?* You went to bed with both of them? At the same time?"

Ryker looked sheepish, and at the same time proud.

"You are my hero, Ryker," Quincy said, "you know that, don't ya?"

"Go to hell," Ryker said.

"Don't worry, friend," Quincy said, sitting in the chair, "your women are safe with me."

"I'll be back in the morning."

"I'll be here," Quincy said. "Does your friend Adams know about me?"

"He does."

"I mean, I don't want to be shot by no living legend Gunsmith in the middle of the night."

"You won't be," Ryker assured him.

"Okay then, you run along and get your beauty rest,"

Quincy said. "You got ladies to impress in the mornin'."

"Never mind what I got to do," Ryker said. "You just keep your eyes open."

"And my pants closed, right?"

"Quincy—"

"That's gonna be hard to do," the bigger man went on. "After all, I am a big, beautiful, black hunk of—"

"Good night, Quincy!"

FORTY-ONE

It was getting dark when Clint spotted Harvey Bell walking down the street.

"There's Bell," he said.

Goodman had taken a seat on the roof and was dozing off. They had decided to take turns on watch. Now he scrambled to his feet and looked over the ledge.

"That's him, all right," the policeman said. "That leaves only John."

"We've got three," Clint said. "Think we should go for four?"

"Clint, my money is on John as the actual killer because of the knife," Goodman said.

"Then we wait for him."

"We got another problem, though," the policeman pointed out.

"Like what?"

"Well, if those three start to leave they'll be long gone by the time we get down from this roof."

"You've got a point," Clint said. "We've got to go back down, then."

"John is not like these fellas, Clint," Goodman said. "He's a pro. He'll spot us."

"Then what do you suggest?"

Goodman rubbed his jaw.

"I don't know yet."

"It's going to be dark soon, as well," Clint said. He was concerned with Goodman's eyesight from up here, and in the dark, but he didn't want the man to know that. "We're going to have a hard time seeing him."

"That's it," Goodman said.

"What is?"

"We should be okay in the doorway when it's dark," Goodman said. "The shadows should hide even me."

"Okay, then," Clint said, "we might as well get down there."

They started away from the roof ledge when Clint thought he saw something on the street. He waited a moment, even when Goodman called out to him.

"Wait—" Clint said.

"What is it?"

"It's him," Clint said, recognizing John.

"What?"

"He's coming down the street right now," Clint said, waving Goodman back to the ledge.

They watched together as John came down the street and entered the saloon.

"Damn, they're all in there," Goodman said. "Let's get the hell down there and get this over with."

"Do you have a gun, Lieutenant?"

"I've got one."

"Can you hit anything with it?"

"Don't you worry, Clint," Goodman said, "I can hit what I aim at."

"Fine," Clint said. "Then let's do it."

FORTY-TWO

Clint and Goodman got down off the roof and crossed the street to stand in front of the saloon. Clint pressed his face to the glass and saw the four men sitting at the table together. They all had beers in front of them.

"They're in there," he said, "all together."

"Let's go," Goodman said.

"Are you doing this officially, Lieutenant?" Clint asked.

"Yes, I am," Goodman said. "I'm going to question them about their whereabouts the night the Frenchman was murdered."

"And if they convince you that they weren't involved?" Clint asked.

"They're guilty of something, Clint," Goodman said. "Their kind always is. I would love to put them away, if not for this murder then for something. Failing that I would like to get them to leave San Francisco."

"But?"

"But if I feel convinced that they're telling the truth

165

and they're not involved, there's nothing I can do to
them.''

"What if I go in the front," Clint asked, "and you go
in the back?"

"And you'll question them?"

"No," Clint said, "I'll just go to the bar and mind my
own business."

"Ah," Goodman said, "you want to see if they make
a move on you."

"If they try to kill me," Clint said, "you can grab them
for that."

"Hell," Goodman said, "if they do kill you I can grab
them for that, too."

"Your concern is touching," Clint said. "Do you want
to do it this way or not?"

"Sure, why not?" Goodman said. "Just give me time
to get to the back door."

"If the place has a back door."

"Don't worry," Goodman said, "if it doesn't I'll come
in a window. Your back will be covered."

"I'm counting on it."

"Just give me a few minutes," Goodman said. "I'll go
down the alley. There's got to be a way to get in the
back."

Goodman disappeared into the alley, and Clint gave
him more than a few minutes to get positioned before
going inside.

It was John who saw Clint as soon as he entered.

"Bell."

"What?"

John jerked his head toward the bar and Bell looked.

"Isn't that the guy on the dock?" Starr asked. He had been the first to arrive in the saloon, the man Clint and Goodman had followed.

"That's him," Bell said, watching Clint walk to the bar. "What the hell is he doin' here?"

"Coincidence?" Lukas asked. His arm in the sling still hurt from the last time they'd met.

"I don't like it," Bell said. He looked around to see if there was anyone else in the room he didn't like.

"We could leave him be," John said.

"I don't think so," Bell said.

"We gonna kill 'im?" Starr asked.

Bell was still looking around.

"I don't see anybody coverin' him," John said.

"I don't either," Bell said, "and that bothers me. Why would he come in here alone?"

"Maybe he ain't afraid," John said.

"Or maybe it's just a coincidence, like I said," Lukas insisted.

"It's no coincidence," Bell said. He looked at John. "This is your call, John. You said from the start that he was a pro, like you."

"He is."

"Then how do we handle him?"

"Carefully," the older man said, "very carefully."

FORTY-THREE

Clint knew the men had seen him. As he stood at the bar with a beer in front of him, he was able to watch them through the mirror. He guessed that they were discussing his entry into the place and whether or not it was coincidence.

"You gonna drink that beer?" the bartender asked Clint.

"What?" Clint asked, because he hadn't heard what the man had said.

"I asked if anythin' was wrong with that beer," the bartender said.

Clint lifted it and tasted it without averting his eyes from the mirror.

"It's fine."

The bartender frowned, then decided that Clint wasn't worth his time. If the man wanted to order a beer and then not drink it, that was his business.

The first one to push his chair back was Starr. He got up slowly and, watching Clint the entire way, walked to the front door and stood there. The next was Lukas, who went and stood next to the back door. Since his right arm was in a sling, he'd be drawing with his left in a cross draw. That meant that Bell and John were going to brace him, which is the way it figured to happen.

Sure enough Bell got up first, followed by John, and they walked to the bar and stood on either side of him.

"Don't we know you?" Bell asked.

Clint took his time. He looked at Bell, and then at John, then back at Bell.

"We've met," he said, "but you don't know me."

"Sure we do," Bell said. "You're the fella likes to put his nose in other people's business."

"Only when the other people are assholes who bother women," Clint said.

"Who you callin' an asshole?" Bell demanded.

"You," Clint said. "Why, you think being called an asshole is something to die over? Go ahead, tough guy. Go for your gun. See where it gets you."

"He's a brave talker," Bell said to John. "Ain't he a brave fella?"

Clint looked at John. The man was wearing a gun, but he'd been told that John's weapon of choice was a knife, so he knew the man had to have one on him somewhere.

"My guess is," Clint said to him, "that you'd rather use a knife on me than that gun. You're a lot better with a knife than with a gun, aren't you, John?"

If John was surprised at the use of his name, he didn't show it. The others were surprised, though.

"How do you know his name?" Bell asked.

"Same way I know that you're Bell," Clint said, without taking his eyes off of John, "the fella by the door is

Starr, and the fella with the broken arm is Lukas."

Three of them didn't like that Clint knew who they were.

"How'd you find out our names?" Bell demanded.

"Hey," Clint said, "you fellas are famous."

"We are?" Starr asked from the door.

The other patrons in the place, sensing that something was about to happen, were all poised to hit the floor at a moment's notice. The bartender was also ready to drop to the floor.

"Sure," Clint said, "the police know all about you. Four small-timers looking for Barbary Coast drunks to roll or women to hassle."

"Who's small-time?" Bell demanded.

"You, Bell," Clint said. He turned his head and looked at the man. "You're small-time—that is, unless you've added murder to your list of talents recently."

"What do you mean, murder?"

"The Frenchman you and your friends were making trouble for the other day? He turned up dead in his hotel room, or didn't you know?" He turned and looked at John. "His throat was cut. You're pretty good at that, I hear."

John studied Clint for a few moments, then asked, "Who are you?"

"My name is Clint Adams."

There was dead silence in the room, and Clint could hear the sound of several men catching their breath sharply. He didn't know who, but somebody recognized the name. From the looks of John, he did, too.

"My name's Harlan John," he said.

"Did you kill the Frenchman, Harlan?"

"We didn't kill nobody," Bell said. "Is that why you're here, Adams? Because you think we killed somebody?"

"A friend of mine," Clint said.

"That Frenchy was a friend of yours?" Bell asked. "I always heard the Gunsmith liked women."

Now there was a surprised sound from those who hadn't recognized his name but recognized him now. Someone even whispered, "The Gunsmith." Clint wondered if it was Starr or Lukas.

"What do you say, Harlan?" Clint asked. "Did you do it?"

"I didn't do it," John said. "I had no reason."

Clint believed the man.

"What are we going to do here, Harlan?" Clint asked. "Somebody going to get killed here?"

John shook his head.

"What about these others?" Clint asked. "They kill the Frenchman?"

"Starr and Lukas, they wouldn't," John said. "They're too stupid to do something like that without bein' told."

"Hey—" Starr said, but didn't follow up on it.

"What about Bell?"

"Don't talk to him, John," Bell said. "Let him talk to me."

Clint said to John, "I'm going to give you my back, Harlan. If you put a knife into it I'm going to be real disappointed in you."

He turned and looked at Bell.

"What about it, Bell?" he asked. "Did you do it?"

"I might have," Bell said. "Yeah, I might have at that. What would you do about it if I said I did?"

"I wouldn't do anything," Clint said, "but there's a policeman here who would."

"You're lyin'," Bell said. "You came alone."

"No, I didn't," Clint said. "I wouldn't be dumb enough to walk in here alone, Bell."

"Bell?" Starr said, after a moment. "What do we do?"

"You think I'm afraid of you because you're the Gunsmith?" Bell asked. "I'm not."

"Good for you."

"None of us are," Bell said.

"Speak for yourself, Bell," John said.

"What?" Bell asked.

"You're a fool if you're not afraid of him," the older man said. "Take my advice. Tell him the truth, and then we'll all walk out of here. Otherwise somebody is gonna get killed."

"I ain't tellin' him nothin'," Bell said. "What do you want to do about it, Gunsmith?"

"I think the question is," Clint said, "what do you want to do about it? I don't think your friends Starr and Lukas want any part of this . . . do you, boys?"

"Bell?" Starr said. "Didn't sign on to face down no Gunsmith. You never said nothin' about that."

"You're a coward, Starr," Bell said.

"That may be."

"What about you, Lukas?" Bell asked. When there was no answer he said again, "Lukas?"

It was John who took a look.

"Lukas is gone, Bell."

"What?" Bell said. He looked and saw that this was true. "That coward ran off!"

"I don't think so," Clint said. "I think my friend the policeman took care of him already."

"You're lyin' about that, Adams!" Bell said. "You're all alone here."

"That may be," Clint said, "but I think you are, too, Bell."

FORTY-FOUR

Ryker went home, but he couldn't sleep. He kept thinking about Jolie. Also, Marie was bothering him a bit. When the three of them had been in bed together Marie had been voracious. Also, she was very competitive with Jolie for his attentions, fiercely so. There was something about the look in Marie's eyes that bothered him.

He finally decided that he couldn't force himself to sleep, so he got up, got dressed, and went back to the Maxwell Hotel.

It was late and the lobby was pretty empty. There was still some gambling going on in the casino, but other than that the hotel seemed deserted. He went upstairs to the second floor, wanting to check on the women. When he got to the hallway he saw that Quincy was not sitting in his chair but was sprawled on the floor.

"Quincy!" he shouted, racing down the hall. He saw that his friend was lying in a pool of blood. It looked like his throat had been cut.

"Jesus," Ryker said, bending over the man.

Then, suddenly, he heard something and saw Quincy's

mouth move. He was still alive!

"Quincy," he said, leaning closer.

"Bitch," Quincy rasped, "crazy bitch . . ."

"Jesus, Quincy," Ryker said, "hang on. Don't die on me, Quincy. Don't die!"

He tore a big piece from his own shirt and tied it around Quincy's throat to stop some of the blood, and then went to find a doctor.

Clint waited for Bell to make some kind of move.

"Come on, Bell," he said. "What's it going to be?"

"John?" Bell said, not taking his eyes from Clint. "Are you with me on this?"

Before the older man could answer, another voice spoke.

"I think you're all alone, Bell," Goodman said. "Starr! Drop your gun on the floor."

Clint couldn't see Goodman but he did see Starr. The man obeyed and seemed relieved to do so.

"John," Goodman said. "You next."

Clint heard John's gun hit the floor.

"And your knife."

Clint heard the knife fall to the floor.

"Okay, Clint," Goodman said, "he's all yours."

"Now's your chance, Bell," Clint said. "Come on, make a name for yourself."

Bell licked his lips, looked past Clint at John and Lieutenant Goodman.

"Well?" Clint asked.

Bell looked at him again, licked his lips, and swallowed hard.

"I didn't kill nobody," Bell muttered.

"What did he say?" Goodman asked.

Clint turned and looked at Goodman.

"He says he didn't kill anybody."

Goodman didn't look happy.

"Ah, shit."

FORTY-FIVE

Clint and Goodman got back to the hotel late, expecting to find it very quiet. Instead they found three men carrying another man down the stairs, with Ryker walking alongside of them.

"What happened?" Clint asked. He noticed that the man being carried was injured and black. Probably Ryker's friend Quincy.

"Somebody cut his throat," Ryker said.

"Is he dead?" Goodman asked.

"No, he's alive," another man said.

"Who are you?" Goodman asked.

"Dr. Hannibal. It's a miracle, but this man is still alive. We must get him to a hospital."

"Why isn't he dead?" Goodman asked.

"Apparently whoever cut his throat was not strong enough to do a thorough job. Now I must go!"

"All right," Goodman said, "go." He looked at Ryker. "Who did it?"

"I don't know."

"Did he say anything?" Clint asked.

"All he said was, 'crazy bitch,' " Ryker said.

"Where are the girls?" Clint asked.

"I don't know."

"They're not here?"

"Not in their rooms," Ryker said hurriedly, casting his eyes toward the door, "and not in yours. Clint, I want to go with Quincy."

"All right, go ahead. Let me know how he is."

"Right."

Ryker ran out the door and Clint turned to Goodman.

"We have to find those women."

"Yes," Goodman said, "I know."

"You're thinking they did it, aren't you?" Clint asked.

"What are you thinking?"

Clint frowned.

"I'm thinking we should find them and ask them," he said.

"I'll send for some men to help us search the area."

"All right," Clint said. "Also the Barbary Coast."

"If they've been taken, why would they be there?" Goodman asked.

"That's where LeConte was killed," Clint said, "and if they're on their own, they might be trying to get on a ship."

"You're right," Goodman said. "All right, the Coast, too."

"While you do that I'll look through the hotel once," Clint said.

"Meet me back here in the lobby," Goodman said.

"Right."

As Goodman went to get his men, Clint decided to

check the second floor again. Maybe they had checked the girls' room but not his. As he headed for the stairway he was intercepted by Morgan, the manager.

"Mr. Adams, this is terrible," he said, wringing his hands.

"Yes, isn't it?"

"When I agreed to help you and the ladies I had no idea something like this would happen—"

"Well, neither did I, Mr. Morgan."

"I mean—well, murder—I don't know what to say—I'm afraid I'll have to, uh, ask you to leave—"

"In the morning, Mr. Morgan," Clint said, patting the man's shoulder. "By morning I'm sure this will all be cleared up."

"Well, I certainly hope so."

"Now, if you'll excuse me," Clint said, "I have to see if I can find the ladies."

As Clint started for the door, Morgan said, "Oh, they're not up there."

"They're not?"

"No."

"How do you know that?"

"I saw them leave."

"And you didn't try to stop them?"

"Why should I have?" he asked. "They were taking one of the girls to the doctor."

"How do you know that?"

"They asked for a cab, and I got them one."

"Did you hear them ask the cab driver to take them to a doctor?"

"Well, no, I didn't hear where they asked him to take them."

"Then how do you know they were going to a doctor?" Clint asked, ready to shake the man.

"Well, they must have been. One of them had blood on her hands."

FORTY-SIX

Clint went out front to try to catch Goodman, but he was too late. He was going to have to do this himself and hope that Goodman would catch up. He hailed a cab and told the driver to take him to the Barbary Coast. They had to be going back there. It was the only other place they knew.

When he got to the Coast, he paid the cab and headed for the hotel the girls had originally stayed in with Henri LeConte. When he got there the lobby was deserted and the desk clerk had his head down on the desk. For a moment Clint thought the man was dead, but then he saw that he was breathing. He didn't bother the man, just bypassed him and went up the stairs. He remembered what room LeConte was in, and what room the girls were in. He didn't think they had gone to LeConte's. He had already searched that room. He went directly to the room they had shared. The door was unlocked and when he opened it the three of them turned and stared at him. They had all been crouched over something on the floor.

"Clint!" Gaby was the first one to recover enough to

181

speak. "Oh, I'm so glad you're here. Those men came to the hotel. They hurt the black man, Quincy. They—"

"What men?"

"What?"

"What men came to the hotel, Gaby?"

"The—the men from the docks. Those men who killed Henri. They came to the hotel—"

"No, they didn't, Gaby."

"What?"

"They didn't come to the hotel. They were with me."

"Wha—they couldn't have been—they—"

"Let me see your hands."

"Who?" Gaby asked.

"All of you," Clint said. "I want to see all of your hands."

"What for?"

"Because I don't think you had time to wash the blood off," Clint said.

They all put their hands behind their backs.

"It really doesn't matter," Clint said. "The police will be here soon."

"The police?" Marie said, looking shocked. "Gaby, you said they wouldn't catch up—"

"Quiet, Marie!" Jolie said.

"She was wrong, Marie," Clint said. "You have been caught. You killed Henri and you tried to kill Quincy tonight. And if I'm not wrong, you also have Henri's money. I should have seen it from the beginning. I searched his room, and it was probably hidden here in your room."

None of them answered.

"I took you away from here so quickly, and I haven't let you be alone since. Tonight, for some reason, you decided to come back for the money. Was Quincy that easy to get by?"

After a moment Gaby said, "No, it was not easy. We had to hold him down. Jolie and I are the strongest, so Marie had to cut his throat."

Marie took her hands out from behind her back now and Clint saw the blood on them.

"That explains why he isn't dead," Clint said. "She didn't have the strength to kill him. That means that Jolie killed Henri, because you were with me, Gaby."

"It doesn't matter which of us held the knife," Gaby said. "We all planned it."

"Why?"

"Because he was a beast, and he deserved to die. He didn't give us any money, and when he did he made us earn it with sex. When those men attacked us on the dock, we saw a chance to kill him and blame them."

Gaby took her hands out from behind her back now and he saw the money in them.

"We could pay you to let us go," Gaby said.

Clint shook his head.

"Take it," Gaby said, holding it out, "take it all."

He shook his head again.

"There's not enough money in the world for me to let you go, Gaby," Clint said.

"Why? Because I slept with you? Do you feel betrayed?"

"No," Clint said, "I feel sad." And the truth of the matter was, he did feel a little used.

Jolie took her hands out from behind her back. She was holding a bloody knife. It looked like the kind of knife sailors used. They had probably gotten it while still on the boat. They had planned LeConte's murder that well.

Clint felt very sad.

"Put the knife on the floor, Jolie."

Jolie hesitated and looked at Gaby.

"Tell her to put it down, Gaby," he said. "Don't make me shoot her."

Gaby studied him and then asked, "You *would* shoot her, wouldn't you?"

"Yes," Clint said, "I would."

Gaby dropped the money onto the floor and told Jolie, "Drop the knife, Jolie."

The black girl did as she was told.

"Gaby?" Marie said. "Are we not going home?"

"No, Marie," Gaby said, "we are not going home."

"Come on, ladies," Clint said, "let's go downstairs and wait for the sheriff."

Watch for

CRIME OF PASSION

169th in the exciting GUNSMITH series
from Jove

Coming in January!

If you enjoyed this book, subscribe now and get...

TWO FREE

A $7.00 VALUE–

If you would like to read more of the very best, most exciting, adventurous, action-packed Westerns being published today, you'll want to subscribe to True Value's Western Home Subscription Service.

Each month the editors of True Value will select the 6 very best Westerns from America's leading publishers for special readers like you. You'll be able to preview these new titles as soon as they are published, *FREE* for ten days with no obligation!

TWO FREE BOOKS

When you subscribe, we'll send you your first month's shipment of the newest and best 6 Westerns for you to preview. With your first shipment, two of these books will be yours as our introductory gift to you absolutely *FREE* (a $7.00 value), regardless of what you decide to do. If

you like them, as much as we think you will, keep all six books but pay for just 4 at the low subscriber rate of just $2.75 each. If you decide to return them, keep 2 of the titles as our gift. No obligation.

Special Subscriber Savings

When you become a True Value subscriber you'll save money several ways. First, all regular monthly selections will be billed at the low subscriber price of just $2.75 each. That's at least a savings of $4.50 each month below the publishers price. Second, there is never any shipping, handling or other hidden charges—*Free home delivery*. What's more there is no minimum number of books you must buy, you may return any selection for full credit and you can cancel your subscription at any time. A TRUE VALUE!